CRAIG HALLORAN

THE SUPERNATURAL BOUNTY HUNTER FILES

SMOKE RISING
BOOK 1

Smoke Rising
The Supernatural Bounty Hunter Series: Book 1
By Craig Halloran

Copyright © 2014 by Craig Halloran
Print Edition

TWO-TEN BOOK PRESS
P.O. Box 4215, Charleston, WV 25364

ISBN eBook: 978-1-941208-11-3
ISBN Paperback: 978-1-941208-12-0

http://www.thedarkslayer.net

Edited by Cherise Kelley

Publisher's Note
This book is a work of fiction. Names, characters, places, and incidents either are the product of the author's imagination or are used fictitiously, and any resemblance to actual persons, living or dead, events, or locales is entirely coincidental.

PROLOGUE

THE MAN-LIKE THING LURCHED UP and smacked Smoke in the chin.

He staggered back.

It started walking down the hall, arms dangling at its sides and a hole clean through its back and chest.

Sidney took aim.

Blam! Blam! Blam!

It tumbled over with its kneecap blasted apart.

"Good shot." Smoke wiped his brow and headed after their fallen attacker where it writhed on the floor. "I think it's a zombie." He pointed his weapon at its head.

Blam!

"Zombies aren't real," she said, catching her breath and holstering her gun.

CHAPTER 1

HUNTSVILLE DETENTION FACILITY, ALABAMA

"ARE YOU NERVOUS?" THE WARDEN asked.

"No," Sidney said. "Why would I be?"

Warden Decker shrugged. Dabbing the sweat on his brow with his handkerchief and tucking it back in his pocket, he hustled forward and swiped his card. Nothing happened. He swiped it again and again. An unseen latch popped.

"Ah, there we go." He opened one of two heavy metal doors and stepped aside. "It's an old place. Not made for all this technology. I miss the sound of those keys jangling on my hip some days."

"Thank you," she said, crossing into the next room.

"You're welcome, Agent Shaw."

The pair entered a long hall made of cinderblock wall, lined with barred windows. Agent Shaw's short heels echoed on the marble floor. The prison was old, but it had the smell of fresh paint that still lingered on the pale grey walls.

The thickset black man cleared his throat. "I've been

the warden these ten years, and I have to admit, I've never had a situation like this."

"Like what?" She adjusted the strap of her black leather satchel on her shoulder.

"We just don't get a lot of visitors from the FBI, that's all. And you have to admit, the situation is very unique." He was smiling as he glanced over at her. "Isn't it?"

"For you, I suppose, but I've been doing this for quite some time."

"Visiting prisoners in sweat-rank prisons?" He huffed. "You didn't sign up for that, did you?" He let out a little laugh. "Sounds more like something a foolish young man would do, like me."

She showed the slightest smile on her face. Dark hair was pinned up behind her head. She wore a dark-blue pants suit with a white shirt. She reminded him of his daughter, in a white sort of way. Too confident for her own good.

"My job requires me to go to a lot of unique places, but I'll admit, Warden Decker, I don't think I've been to a place as humid as this."

"They've been working on the A/C for twenty years, and it still never works right. I'm from the South, and I still never get used to it." He dashed the sweat from his eyes. "Sorry. But this hallway has no ventilation at all."

"It's all right. The academy's prepared me for worse."

He stopped at the next set of doors, readied his swipe key, and paused.

She dipped her chin and eyed him. "Something on your mind, Warden?"

He leaned on the door, took out his blue handkerchief, and wiped his neck. "I just got to know. Why do you need to see him?"

"That's confidential."

"I know that, but... it's so strange. Listen, Agent Shaw. I'm the warden. Certainly you can give me some nugget of information. After all, he's my prisoner. I'm pretty familiar with him. I'm pretty familiar with all of them. We have the worst of all sorts here: dangerous maniacal bloodthirsty killers. Of course, I've seen some of them cry like babies before." He gave her a quick finger shake. "But we don't have—and never have had—anyone like him."

"Sorry," she said, looking at the next set of doors.

They were painted white, with the word "LIBRARY" stenciled in black where the window glass had been replaced with steel.

"Is this really a library?"

"It is." He tapped on the metal. "This is how we make do. I don't think we get the same level of funding as the G-Men"—he looked her up and down—"or G-Women do. Are you sure I can't stay inside with you?"

"I'll be fine." She shifted her satchel from one side to the other.

He took a breath and swiped his card. "All right then."

CHAPTER 2

T HE LATCH POPPED, AND THE warden pushed the door open. It was a library as expected, with stacks and rows of books. The musty smell reminded Sidney of her days in high school. She'd done a lot of reading back then. Large wooden tables were lined up neatly, resting on old hardwood floors.

Two correction officers in grey shirts and black pants held synthetic stocked shotguns on either side of a table. A man in an orange jumper sat there between them. His head was down over a newspaper and his dark straight hair dangled over his face.

Her heart thumped behind her temples.

"I can stay inside, just out of earshot," the warden said, patting the semiautomatic pistol on his hip.

She lifted a brow. "I don't think he'll try to escape, or even to hurt me, for that matter. It's not in his profile."

The warden blocked her view of the prisoner and whispered, "I've read his profile too. Several times. He has a dark side to him."

"I know, but don't all men?"

Warden Decker nodded and stepped aside. "Come on, men." But at the last second, he turned to her and said, gradually getting loud enough for the prisoner to hear, "As long as you stay out of the stacks, I've got eyes on everything. Just signal when you're finished."

The guards came forward, eyeing her as they passed the threshold.

"Uh, Warden—"

Warden Decker held his hand up and led them out.

Sidney glanced over her shoulder as the doors began to close, just in time to see Warden Decker swallow. Her heart skipped a beat as the door sealed shut. She turned and faced the prisoner.

Pull it together. He's just another creep, Sidney.

She approached him, heart thumping. It was even hotter in the library, and she could feel the sweat beading above her lip. Her eyes slid toward the camera globes above. *Those things better be on.* She dropped her file on the table, dragged a chair back, and sat down. The man across from her, eyes still down, turned a page of the newspaper.

"John Smoke," she said, scooting her file in front of her and opening it. "I'm Agent Shaw with the FBI. How are you doing today?"

Without glancing up, he said, "You're different than what I expected. What are you, about five foot eleven? That's tall for a gal. And you're even wearing flat shoes. The last one I met was a sawed-off dumpling with Coke-bottle glasses. I didn't like her so well." He scanned the paper, turned the last page, folded it up, and pushed it aside. He clasped his fingers together and looked down into her eyes. "Volleyball. I bet you played collegiate volleyball."

Smoke was hawkish, but handsome. His chestnut hair was thick and cut just above the neck. His eyes were dark with a burning fire behind them. He was a strong-chinned, lean, well-knit man with hands the size of mitts.

"This is business, Mister Smoke, not a social call."

"You know"—he eased back in his chair—"you aren't exactly what I figured for an FBI woman. I was expecting someone a little less, well, a lot less—to keep it professional— appealing. I have to say, it's a nice surprise." He scratched the scruff on his cheeks. "Shaw. Is that your maiden name?"

Sidney didn't have a ring on. "I'll ask the questions. You just answer them."

"Well, you haven't asked anything yet." His voice was a little rough, with a hair of charm behind it. He clasped his fingers together and rested them on his head. "I'm all yours."

"All right, Mister Smoke—"

"Smoke," he interrupted.

"Excuse me?"

"Just call me Smoke." He winked. "That's what everyone calls me."

"Sure," she said. "First question then. Are you interested in getting your sentence commuted?"

He shrugged.

I'm starting to hate this guy. Sidney had interviewed dozens of prisoners over her career. She'd negotiated deals with many. Every time she mentioned someone getting their sentence commuted, their eyes lit up. Smoke's hadn't.

"You're less than a year into a three-year sentence," she continued. "And when I say commute, I'm not talking about months off. I'm talking about years."

Rubbing a bruise on his cheek just below the ear, he said, "I've become pretty fond of the old place." He glanced around. "It speaks to me."

"Warden Decker says you and the other prisoners don't get along so well."

"He's such a worrywart. Nice guy, though."

"I'm been informed that there's a bounty on your head." She leaned forward. "In most cases, the superior numbers get you. One slip-up or payoff of the guards will get you killed in here."

"It keeps me sharp," he said.

"Getting killed?"

"People trying to kill you is always the best training."

"I see," she said. "And I guess I shouldn't be surprised after reading your file." She leafed through some pages. "You've had quite a career for a man under thirty. Navy SEAL. Ex-Washington PD. Bounty Hunter. Prisoner. Now that's a resume."

"Chicks dig it."

"There aren't any *chicks* around here, and there won't be for the next two years. The funny thing I came across is how you wound up here in the first place. You are a decorated veteran, though not without some marks. Tell me, why'd you leave the SEALs?"

"I didn't like the pay."

"Oh, the pay," she said, eyeing the file and nodding, "but that's not what it says here. The gist I got was that you are difficult to control. Insubordinate. You struck an officer."

"He had a big mouth."

"He was a general."

"He had a really big mouth." He shrugged. "And I got an honorable discharge. I hope you read that far."

"I see," she said. "So you didn't like the military?"

"Listen, Agent Shaw. I loved the military. But there is a lot of standing around, training, and waiting. I got bored."

"It doesn't say that here."

"Do you believe everything you read?"

Interesting. But at least he's talking. "Let's skip over the Washington PD and talk about why you became a bounty hunter."

"Better money."

"Really? So you're all about the money?"

"Yes."

"I don't believe you."

"I don't care."

Typical stubborn man.

"Fine. Let's talk money then. The last goon you brought in was worth ten thousand."

"It should have been fifty, and I still haven't received payment for that."

"No?" Sidney said, cocking her head. "Well, I wonder why *that* is?"

Smoke looked away and growled in his throat a little. He mumbled something.

Sidney leaned forward and turned her ear toward him. "What was that?"

The room seemed to darken when Smoke's eyes narrowed. He slammed his fist on the table. *Wham!* "He had it coming!"

CHAPTER 3

HEART RACING, SIDNEY FLINCHED BACK. Smoke's eyes were smoldering fires. Behind her, the doors burst open, and two guards dashed in. The first one drove the butt of his shotgun into Smoke's chest, toppling him over. In a second, both barrels were lowered toward his chest.

"Don't you move, Smoke," the first guard said. "Not an inch."

"Are you all right, Miss?"

Face flushed red, Sidney jumped from her chair. "Get your sorry asses out of here!"

"What?"

"Did I signal for the cavalry?"

"Well…"

"Did I?" She pointed at the cameras.

"But—" the first guard started.

"Jeff," a voice shouted from just outside the library doors. "Moe! Let's go!" It was Warden Decker. His chest was heaving and his face beaded in sweat. He loosened his tie. "Now!"

With hesitation, the guards lifted their barrels and backed off, eyes never leaving Smoke.

"Sorry, Miss."

Sidney glared at him.

"Er… Sorry, Agent Shaw."

Sidney waved the warden off, and he showed her a squeamish grin. Seconds later, the doors closed again, leaving her all alone with Smoke. She turned and found him in the chair, with a slight smile on his face. She hid a gasp. She hadn't even heard him move. No rattle of metal nor scuff of chair. Nothing. She resumed her seat.

"How's your chest? I bet that hurt."

"I've been hurt worse." His eyes were dancing. "You're prior military too, aren't you?"

"Let's pick up where we left off before you had your little tantrum, shall we? I believe you were saying you're upset that you haven't been paid."

"I took a major thug off the streets. A top dealer." He rolled his shoulders and grimaced a little. "I should have been paid. I was tossed in here instead."

"The judge didn't see it that way." She glanced through the file. "It says you acted with extreme prejudice."

"The man's a killer. A murderer."

"That's for the courts to decide. And we can't just go around maiming people."

Smoke lifted his brows. "Even if it saves a life?"

"You cut off his index finger."

"No, I cut off his trigger finger."

She wanted to laugh but held it back. "Most people only have one trigger finger. You cut off two."

"I can shoot right- or left-handed. Can't you?"

"I've never had the need. As for you, well, I'd venture to guess your little act of mutilation didn't sit well with Mister Durn. That's probably why he put the prison hit on you."

"Huh, well, I've been a bounty hunter a long time."

"You've been one four years."

"That's a long time." He crinkled his brow. "Anyway, I've achieved a lot in that time. Helped a lot of people. But some of those judges aren't so helpful. Durn has deep pockets. It's no surprise he paid the judge off and got me sent inside here."

"Maybe the judge was coerced."

"He should be willing to die first."

Sidney nodded. Smoke had a point, but it was all speculation. She picked up the file and fanned herself with it.

"It's in the past now. Let's talk about the future. Are you interested in hearing what I have to offer or not?"

He shrugged.

"Yes or no, if you please."

"Does it involve working with the FBI or any other law enforcement agency?"

"Absolutely."

"Then no."

"Why?"

"You've read my file. I don't play well with others. Too many rules. Not enough action. That's why the bad guys get away. Besides, I don't trust them. If I did, I'd probably be doing what you're doing."

"Come on." She leaned back. "We aren't all bad."

"See, you just admitted it."

17

"Admitted what?"

"That most of you are bad." He tilted his head back and let out a laugh. "Hah."

"That's a common expression."

"Says the girl scout. And I bet you think those cookies you're selling are good for me, too." He shook his head. "No one is as blind as he who will not see."

"My eyes are wide open."

"I'm sure they are, but my answer is still no."

"So, you'd rather sit in here for two more years plus and let more criminals get away?"

"There are plenty of criminals inside here that are in need of my correction."

Difficult. Difficult. Difficult. The man across from her seemed content, however. It was weird.

"So long as I'm here, will you just listen to my offer?" He shrugged. "Sure."

"The FBI has a list." She clasped her hands together and rested them on the table. "The typical America's Most Wanted. You're familiar with it, I'm sure."

"Uh-huh. Say, what kind of perfume are you wearing?" He sniffed the air. "It's different. Good, but different."

"The Marshalls have their lists. The Washington PD has their lists too," she continued, "more on the local level. You've dealt with them all, and disregarding the last case, you've done an exemplary job."

"Yeah." He yawned and eased back until he lifted the front legs of his chair from the floor, then started gazing around. "I know all of the lists. It's what I do."

"But there's another list, one that isn't on the public record. It's called—"

Smoke's brows lifted, and his chair legs hit the floor. He leaned over the table and spoke.

"The Black Slate."

CHAPTER 4

I'VE GOT HIM.

"Let me see the list," Smoke said, unable to hide the excitement in his voice. "I knew it existed."

"Oh, did you now? You don't sound so sure."

"It was a theory."

"Based off what? The Black Slate has very little activity. It's very low profile."

"True, but I know all the lists pretty well. I've studied the cases, the files, at least whatever I could get ahold of. But there was always something missing. I don't look for what they show or say, I look for what they don't show or say." He drummed his fingers on the table and stared at the file. "All of those lists I figured were nothing but busywork that hid the real people. Good for the papers. Good for accolades and medals. But they never bring in the top-dog criminals." He stretched his fingers toward the file. "May I?"

Sidney slid the file away. She wanted to give it to him, he seemed so eager, child-like even.

"Not without clearance, and I don't see that

happening if you aren't on board with this. Don't fret it. The list isn't in here, just the first assignment. Are you interested or not?"

Smoke pulled his fingers back. "Tell me more. I'm curious. Why does the FBI want to use me as a resource?"

"All right, I can answer that. Let's just say that our resources are stretched thin. Even though the Black Slate, as you call it, is important, other matters have higher priority: border security, domestic terrorism, cyber-attacks, white collar crime. There are only so many agents, and they can only keep tabs on so many things."

"Sure, sure, and I'm supposed to believe the NSA doesn't keep tabs on any of these things? Don't you share information with each other?"

"Like I said, the FBI has priorities, but the Black Slate is still a threat, it just isn't as high up on DC's agenda."

"Ah," Smoke said, "Washington DC, home of the greatest truths and the greatest lies."

"You have a skewed outlook on things," she said. "Where does all this come from?"

"I read a lot of books."

"What kind of books?"

"The kind that aren't on the bestseller lists."

"I see." She nodded. "Is there anything you care to recommend?"

"Nope." Smoke's chair groaned as he shifted. "So this character on the wanted list, tell me about him. Has the FBI tried to catch him?"

"Yes, for years and without success. I've studied the file. We've gotten close, only to see him slip from our grasp time and time again. And these are veteran agents. They speak as if he's a ghost or something."

Smoke tilted his head. "Maybe he is?"

"I don't think so."

"Maybe he's like Bruce Lee and they just can't handle him?" He made some quick chops with his hands. "Wah-tah!"

"I'm certain that's not the case, but several agents were wounded in hand-to-hand combat."

Smoke's eyes widened. "Maybe it's the ghost of Bruce Lee?"

"You are a strange man."

"So, do you have a picture? A name?"

"Are you in?"

Smoke beckoned with his fingers.

Sidney pulled a picture from the file and shoved it over. It was a surveillance shot of a small dark-haired man in a blue suit, stepping out of an SUV. "His name is Vaughn, Adam Vaughn. They call him AV."

Smoke's brows buckled as he studied the picture.

"Is this the only picture you have?"

"The only one on me, and it's the best one we have."

"This guy's about five foot five. Hmmm, and he almost has the unibrow thing going. Spanish descent. Sharp features. Hard-eyed." He rubbed his chin. "Where's the last place they cornered him?"

"DC."

"And what is he suspected of?"

"Trafficking."

"Trafficking what?"

"Everything."

"So you have testimonials?"

"Some living and some dead."

Smoke shoved the picture back across the table.

"All right."

"All right. Does that mean you're in?"

"No, all right as in I'm thinking about it."

CHAPTER 5

SIDNEY JOGGED THE MONUMENTS ROUTE in DC. She checked her watch and heart rate. She was thirty minutes into the run, and her thighs and legs were starting to burn.

Thirty more to go.

It was Saturday, mid-morning, and the sun almost warmed the fall air. She hated running when it was too cold. She didn't like getting up early either, not on Saturday. There were other tasks at home she liked to do. But today was different. This wasn't her usual route or scene. She had another meeting. Her former boss wanted to meet. Outside the office. Privately. First time for everything.

Wiping the sleeve of her grey hoodie across her brow and picking up the pace, she passed two joggers, older, wearing 80s Adidas leisure. She smiled as she ran by. They probably moved much faster thirty years ago. She jogged by several people, strollers, tourists. It wasn't the best time to run, but she liked the extra work that came with running through the slow masses. She picked up on things.

A man sitting on a bench wearing a leisure suit and winding his watch. A group of older women walking at a brisk pace and laughing. One had purple leggings on. Another straightened her red wig from time to time.

She weaved her way around the reflecting pool three more times. Her lungs labored, and her feet burned. She checked her time, pushed on, passed the World War II Memorial and sprinted across the street toward the Washington monument, where she slowed to a walk. Hands on her hips, she strolled toward the monument until she saw a man sitting on a bench, waving.

"Sid! Sid!"

Soaked in sweat, she trotted over. He stood up and opened his arms wide. He was as tall as her, broad and heavy, balding with a handsome smile on his face. She stopped short of him.

"I'm soaked in sweat."

"It's all right," he said in a comforting voice, "I have my raincoat on. Come here."

She sighed and made her way into his arms, which braced her in a bear hug, taking more wind from her. "Easy now, Ted." She patted his back.

"Sorry." He released her. He was still smiling. "I've missed my favorite trooper. It's been awhile." He clasped her hands and held them tight. "You look great."

"Sure I do," she said, brushing the damp hair from her eyes. "You look great yourself."

He patted his stomach. "Maybe twenty, thirty, forty pounds ago." He lumbered back to his seat and sat down with a groan. He patted the bench. "The desk and meetings are killing me."

"Are you sure it isn't the burgers and French fries?" She took a seat.

"It's those buffets at the lunch meetings, I swear it. Marge keeps me on a strict diet." He scratched the top of his head and squinted one eye. "But that diet's not very tasty. Salad, salad and more salad. I try, but I can't figure it out."

"Maybe you should start running again, like we used to."

"Ah," he nodded, "I miss that. Well, your company, not so much the running."

His full name was Ted C. Howard, and Sidney still didn't know what the C stood for. He was the first assistant director she'd worked for. Over fifty years old now, Ted still had the thick-set frame of his football days that he always loved to talk about. He was a good man. Energetic. A good mentor. He'd taught her a little about everything—and a lot about little, when he started to ramble. He was like family. An uncle of sorts.

"So, how was Alabama?" he asked.

"Hot."

"Good country down there," he said. "Nice fishing. Nice people."

"Not where I was," she said, smiling. She bent over and redid the laces on her shoes. "But I'm sure you'd find good company."

"True," he said. "Did I ever tell you about the last time I was down there? I was thirty-nine and…"

Aw crap. Here we go. Cut him off before you end up in tomorrow.

"Yes, you told me," she interrupted. Maybe Ted had

told the story, and maybe he hadn't, but she was pretty sure she'd heard them all. Some of them two or three times, as he'd told them to other people when she was around. "What's this about, Ted?"

"Oh." He seemed disappointed. "How'd your interview with Mister Smoke go?"

Cocking her head, she looked him in the eye. "You know about that?" All she had told him was that she'd come back from Alabama. She hadn't mentioned anything about anyone she'd met.

"I spoke with Warden Decker. We go way back."

"Of course you do." Ted had a catalog of contacts. He had access. If he wanted to know something, he'd find it. "And does your office have an interest in my case? I thought you were handling more of the border cases."

Ted reached into the pocket of his navy trench coat and pulled out a paper bag. It was full of nuts. He tossed one toward the nearest squirrel that was skirting by.

"I'm not keeping tabs on you, Sid, but I have checked up on you from time to time." He flicked another nut out. "But this was different. A little bird dropped me a wire of peculiar interest. I felt compelled to look into it."

"And?"

"The Black Slate. I know a little something about that." The creases deepened over his eyes. "I don't like the idea of you working on this. The way they're going about it is peculiar. It seems... dangerous."

Ted had never been like this before, and they'd navigated some dangerous waters. Why the concern now?

"Danger's part of the job. You told me that."

He laughed. "I think that's a quote from a movie. It's true, but probably much shorter and more eloquent than I would have put it." He flung out a few more nuts where many squirrels had now gathered. "Don't take me wrong. You're as fit to do this as any. If I was in the field, I'd want a piece of the action too." He groaned. "Don't ever get promoted, Sid. They anchor you with cinderblocks to that desk. I should have been a cop. Did I ever tell you—"

She grabbed his shoulder. "Back to the Black Slate, please. John Smoke? You wanted to talk about him."

"Yes, John Smoke. Now that's an odd one. A good candidate on the surface, but all the paperwork below the surface is blacked out or missing."

"You mean I didn't get the entire file?"

"You got enough. I got a little more. That's why I talked to Warden Decker." He pointed at the squirrels. "Look at them. I haven't done this in years. Crazy little rodents. I met a man once who had a squirrel living in the hood of his hoodie. It was after Hurricane Hugo hit Charleston. Construction guy. One of the strangest things I ever saw." He turned and smiled at her. "In a good way."

She glared at him.

"Sorry." He flung the rest of the nuts aside and dusted his hands off. "Truth. Warden Decker likes the guy. But, we aren't the only people taking an interest in him. Decker clammed up when I prodded him. Leaves me uneasy."

"Well, Smoke has neither accepted nor declined my offer, so maybe there's nothing to worry about."

"Interesting, but I assume he'll take it."

"Why's that?"

"I just have a feeling. That said, be careful. I did some deeper research on similar projects like this that failed. The Black Slate is marred with a dark history. They've tried mercs, bounty hunters, and others of their ilk before."

"And what happened? It didn't work out?"

"They're dead. Some, not to mention many of our agents—who aren't even in that file you were toting—are gone without a trace." He peered up at the Washington Monument. "I don't like this, Sid. Just use extraordinary caution." He got up and extended his hand. She took it, and he pulled her up with ease. "I'm serious." He patted her shoulder and started to walk away. He stopped and turned. "Say, how's the Hellcat doing?"

Unable to contain her smile, she said, "Doing great."

"Hah. You stole her from me. I'll never forget that." Moving on, he waved. "Call me if you need anything."

"Good seeing you, Ted. And thanks."

I think.

CHAPTER 6

SIDNEY'S EYES POPPED OPEN. SHE rolled over and grabbed her buzzing phone. Sitting up in bed, blinking, she read the screen. There was an address. A time. And the text came from her supervisor, Dydeck.

"Are you shitting me?" She checked the time. 4:30 a.m. She groaned and fell back into her goose-down pillows. "What does he want now?" she mumbled. "Ugh. Why does he get up so early? Why does he feel compelled to bother me? So early!"

Her toes touched the cold hardwood floor, and she crept into the bathroom and started the shower. The small bath steamed up quick, and into the hot water she went and soaked it up. Five minutes later she was out, drying off, and on the go. She tore the plastic off her dry-cleaned clothes. Seconds later, she had everything on but her shoes and headed for the kitchen.

The studio apartment west of Reston, Virginia didn't offer much. Its eight hundred square feet was furnished from secondhand shops and goodwill stores. A mid-size bed, a small sofa, recliner and a kitchenette with two stools under the bar.

She turned on the television and followed the blurbs on the news. It was Monday. Forty-five degrees and a rainstorm was coming.

"Great."

She grabbed the blender out of the sink and loaded it with ice, protein mix, two eggs, fresh veggies and ice and blended it all up. Eyes intent on the news, she poured the mixture into a travel mug and rinsed the blender out before abandoning it in the sink. She snatched her bag from the kitchen bar, clicked the television off, and headed for the front door. She opened it and stopped. Something didn't feel right. He fingers fell to her waist.

"Ah!"

She shuffled back to the bed and grabbed her weapon from under the pillow. A Glock 22. .40 S&W. Inside her closet, she took her shoulder holster and strapped it on. She paused, staring into the small closet. Another pistol and shoulder holster hung ready. What Ted had said hung in her thoughts. *Use extraordinary caution.* It was a strange phrase. The way he'd said it even more so. At 4:42 am, she was inside an FBI-issued Crown Victoria and rolling down the road. Fifteen minutes into the ride, the rain started in heavy splatters on the windshield. She turned on the wipers, which left streaks of rain, and the defroster wasn't working well either. She wiped the condensation with her hand and sighed. The rising sun was a blur in her eyes. She slipped on her sunglasses.

It's going to be a long week.

While she drove down the road, Sidney's thoughts were heavy. Typically, she headed into the office at 8 a.m. She'd push paperwork for a few hours then go to meetings and briefings. That was seventy percent of the job, maybe eighty. The rest of the time she was in the field. When Dydeck called her out in the field, it could mean anything. Homicide. Drug busts. Stake outs. Talking to clients and informants. Anything dealing with problems or potential problems at the federal level. From time to time they were a cleanup crew of sorts, when the local brass of Washington got their hands too dirty. It was a part of the job she didn't care for.

Two hours later and south of DC, she exited the highway and entered a residential neighborhood along the Potomac.

Homicide?

Dydeck liked to surprise her. He was good about that. He had a way of working them into a little bit of everything, which she liked. Most of the agents were assigned to a particular unit, but Sidney floated along the rim, where the full range of her talents could be put to use. She was classified as special field ops. Not to mention her paperwork. She was thorough, her wording in sync just the way the top brass liked it. The Bureau loved paperwork. Without it, they'd eliminate most of what they did. She hated it.

Her brakes squeaked to a halt as she parked in the driveway of a contemporary one-level home in a lower-middle-class neighborhood. A For Sale sign was in the yard, and there were also signs in the other two yards at the end of the cul-de-sac. Two other cars were there, black SUVs.

Why don't I have one of those?

Through the rain, she could make out one man on the porch in a dark trench coat, standing by the door. She didn't know him.

Aw, great.

No uniformed local law enforcement. That ruled out homicide, but she'd been to plenty of these scenes before. The estranged family members or children of Washington's finest often wound up in dark places: overdoses, suicide, domestic squabbles. The FBI often covered it up before the news outlets caught wind of it.

She grabbed her gear, popped open the door, and dashed through the sloppy wet grass and onto the covered porch.

"Agent Shaw?" the stocky man said, smiling. He had a warmth about him.

She showed her ID.

He glanced at it. "Lousy morning, isn't it."

"You bet."

"I'm Tommy," he said, extending his hand. "Nice to meet you."

She shook it.

"You too."

He opened the door. "They're all waiting for you."

Inside, the house was dimly lit by a lone floor lamp in the living room. There, three men in dark suits waited. Sitting on the large raised hearth was a fourth man in an orange jumpsuit, shackled with his head down.

"Welcome, Sidney," said a man standing off in the corner and putting away his phone. He was in his forties, well-knit, with his head shaven. His eyes slid over to Smoke and back to her. "Well, what do you think?"

"I have to admit, I'm surprised, Jack. And I'm not even including the location. I was under the impression this would be handled downtown. Aren't we outside of protocol?"

"Yes and no. All the paperwork is covered on my end. On the prison end. At the assistant director's end. But hey, it's the list. We have to keep it low." He scratched his head. "And I have to admit, I didn't even know there was a list until a month ago. Huh. Gum?"

"No thanks." She folded her arms over her chest. "So, where do we stand? I'm not really familiar with running things without explicit directives."

"I know that." He nodded to one of the other agents. The man handed another file over. "The directives are in here. Everything we have on the mark as well, including his last known location." He approached and brushed his shoulder against hers. Tapped the file. "Never seen anything like this in twenty years, plucking a low-life out of the prisons to do our job." He sneered at Smoke. "You have two weeks, pal, and then it's back in the hole." He winked at Sidney. "If he gives you any crap, just call and we'll cut this silly mission short." He walked over to Smoke and kicked the man's foot with his boot. "Mind yourself."

The door opened, and another man in a trench coat entered, holding a newspaper over his head with one hand and a briefcase in the other. The man was slender and stoop shouldered, and he wore glasses that looked too heavy for his nose. His frosty eyes met hers.

"Agent Shaw, what a displeasure."

"Agree, Agent Tweel. I couldn't be less happy to see you."

Agent Cyrus Tweel didn't look like much, but he was proven. Sidney had graduated from the academy with him.

Agent Tweel dropped to a knee and popped his briefcase open. "Let's get on with this, shall we? I have more important things to do than waste time on experiments."

Smoke's head tilted up. His gaze fell on Cyrus.

"Jack," Sidney said, "What's going on here?"

"Tracking," Jack said. "We can't lose sight of him. Not for a second. Surely you know that."

Cyrus held up a two-inch needled syringe filled with clear liquid. He flicked it with his fingers.

Smoke rose to his feet. "No one is going to Snake Plissken me!"

"You'll do what you agreed to," Jack said. He nodded to the other agents, who seized Smoke by the arms. "Now be still." Jack pulled out a stun gun. "Or it'll be my pleasure to use this on you."

"No!" Smoke said, struggling against the agents. "No!"

CHAPTER 7

"**T**HAT NEEDLE BETTER NOT GET within a foot of me!" Smoke said.

"What's going on here, Jack?" Sidney said. "What the hell is in there?"

"Something new," Jack said. He pointed to Smoke. "You agreed to this. You better settle yourself."

"I didn't agree to any injections! Screw this! Put me back in prison."

"Jack!" Sidney said, stepping in front of him. "What is it?"

"A vaccination."

"No one is giving me any shots!" Standing taller than the rest, hands cuffed behind his back, Smoke squatted down and drove his shoulder into the agent on his left. The man teetered over but held on, dragging the three of them down in a heap.

"You're going to regret that," Jack said. He stepped around Sidney and pointed the stun gun at Smoke. "I don't have time for this."

Sidney shoved his hand aside.

Jack misfired. The taser prods buried themselves in one of the agents. He jerked, spasmed, and writhed on the floor.

"Dammit, Sid! What did you do that for?"

"This isn't protocol!"

"It is. Read the file. I tell you it is." He shoved by Sidney and drove his toe into Smoke's gut.

"Oof!"

"Settle down, hot dog! Take your medicine!" Jack said. He put his knee on Smoke's neck. "Cyrus!"

Smoke bucked and squirmed.

Zap!

Smoke jerked and writhed.

Behind Sidney, Cyrus had tased him.

"Give him more juice," Jack said. "He's still squirming."

"Gladly," Cyrus said, squeezing the trigger.

Pop. Pop. Pop.

Smoke screamed out, "Aaargh!" A second later he collapsed on the floor, disheveled and coated in sweat.

"Whew!" Jack said, getting up. He ran his forearm across his brow. "What is that man made of?" He helped up the agent who'd caught some juice from his taser. "Sorry about that." He let out a heavy sigh. "Agent Shaw, I'm letting this incident go. But if you ever act insubordinate again, I'll black mark your file."

"But Jack—"

He stepped up to her.

"But Sir!"

He reached into his pocket and grabbed a handkerchief. "Get in line, or I'll withdraw my consideration."

37

Sidney started to say, *Yes, Sir*, but held her tongue.

"You go right ahead, *Sir*. This entire incident is way out of bounds."

"No, you're out of bounds, Sid."

"I'm not the one who lost control of this situation. That's on you, not me. That's no way to treat a person. He's a decorated veteran."

"He *was* a decorated veteran. Now he is some ex-con vigilante hot dog idiot."

She glanced at Smoke. Cyrus was driving the needle into him. "Hey!"

"Back off, Sid," Jack said. "Tohms! Yo, Tommy!"

The man she'd met outside came in.

"What the hell are you doing out there? Didn't you hear the racket?"

"Er..."

"Never mind," Jack said. "Just help Muldoon to the car. He's shaken up."

"Right," Tommie said. He glanced at Sid. There was a bit of sympathy in his eyes. He mumbled as he passed. "Cyrus is an a-hole."

"I heard that," Cyrus said.

"Good," Tommy replied. He helped Muldoon back outside, closing the door behind him.

Jack raised his palms up. "Let's start over. The vaccination. I had to do it. Orders. And that's all I know. It's a vaccination."

"Is there something wrong with him?" Sid said.

"Well, I'm just assuming it's for your protection... and his."

Smoke groaned on the floor.

Cyrus locked an ankle tracker on him.

"Who's keeping tabs on him," Sid said, "me or you?"

"Check your phone?" Cyrus said. "There's an app you need to download. Twenty four seven location. Just don't let your phone go dead. Don't lose it like the last time, either."

"Shut up, Cyrus."

"Listen, Sid," Jack intervened. "This is a strange case. I have my orders. You have yours. Execute them, and I'm sure it will all make sense after everything hashes out. Got it?"

"Sure, I got it."

"Good."

"So," Sid said, "is this headquarters?"

He pointed to a peg on the wall.

"Those are the keys. You can work out of here, or you can work out of his place."

"I'm sure she'd like to take him back to her place." Cyrus snapped his briefcase shut. "Probably why she took the assignment. She always had a thing for damaged guys."

"Cyrus, get going," Jack said.

Agent Tweel departed with a frown, slamming the door behind him. That left only Jack, Smoke, the other agent, and herself in the room.

"Get the car warmed up, Danny," Jack said.

That left only three.

"Sid, I'm sorry for how this went down. You're my best. You know that. But I can't have you questioning me in front of others. Not like that. Respect the chain."

"I know, but—"

"No, the only butt I'm going to have is yours if you cross that line again. Capisce?"

She nodded.

"Good." His eyes slid over to Smoke and back. "I don't know what to make of this. He's all yours though. Read the file. Stay away from the office. Don't hesitate to call. In two weeks this will all be over. Things will be back to normal."

"You say that as if you don't think we can bring this guy in."

"Well, the odds are against you. I'm told no one has ever brought one in. And by the look of things, I don't see that changing." He squeezed her shoulder. "Good luck, Sid."

She could feel his heavy gaze on her back as he headed for the door. It sent a chill through her. She didn't turn.

"Goodbye, Sir."

CHAPTER 8

S ID PEEKED OUT THE CURTAIN in the bay window and watched the black SUV back out of the driveway and roll out. The chill between her shoulders didn't ease. It seemed everyone knew something they weren't telling. First her old boss, Ted, and now her current boss, Jack.

Behind her, metal clanked on the floor.

In a single motion, she spun around and ripped her pistol out. Smoke sat on the hearth, undoing the cuffs on his ankles.

"Freeze!"

He didn't move a muscle.

"Key. Toss it over to me."

He flicked it at her feet. "You don't think I can work shackled and with this prison garb on, do you?"

"No." She holstered her weapon. "But I won't have you playing pickpocket either. Just be still." She gave him a once-over. A moment ago, he'd been completely disheveled, and now he seemed perfectly fine. He should have been laid out still. "Are you all right?"

Smoke nodded. "Maybe a little achy, but that's more from the vaccination than the taser."

"I don't know what that's about."

"Don't worry about it."

She cocked her head. "You seemed pretty upset about it, and now you're not worried."

"Nope."

"So that was a show?"

"Yep." He held his arms out. "Can you please unlock these?"

"So, you know what the shot was?"

"Yep."

"And they don't?"

"That's right."

"Are you going to tell me?"

"Are you going to take these cuffs off?"

"Answer my question first."

"No, I'm not going to tell you what the shot was for. But I will tell you I have a condition. Nothing contagious, but I've had that shot before."

"Who makes those shots?"

"Don't worry about it." He extended his wrists. "It's just a thing. A private thing. I have my right to privacy, you know."

She tossed him the key.

What in the world is going on?

Smoke had been injected with something, and he was the only one who knew what. He had a fit and had taken a walloping for it. Someone beyond pay grades was overseeing this. Watching Smoke. And so far, everything that was going on made absolutely no sense to her.

Smoked unlocked the last set of cuffs and tossed them on the floor. He unzipped his jumpsuit and slipped out of it.

"What are you doing?" she said, averting her eyes. Her glance revealed his lean body was packed with hard muscle.

"Changing," he said, walking over and grabbing a duffle bag in the corner. He emptied the contents of his bag and slipped on a pair of jeans, a black t-shirt, and work boots. "So, you and Cyrus have a past." He repacked the bag and threw in the jumpsuit. "He doesn't seem like your type."

"I beg your pardon?"

Smoke tossed his duffle bag on the counter. "Aw, come on. It's obvious you two dated. But I can't imagine why you broke it off. He seemed so... charming. Beady eyes and all."

"You have wonderful powers of perception." She opened the file and set it on the kitchen table. "But if it's not related to this case, keep it to yourself."

"Sure." He walked over and stood by her side. "But tell me, why did you go out with him? Let me guess: you thought his drive and intelligence outweighed his meager frame and uber-bland personality."

"No." She kept her eyes on the papers in the file.

"You have a thing for short guys?"

"Mister Smoke—"

"Smoke." He smiled. "Just call me Smoke."

"Grab a chair."

Smoke took a seat and hitched one booted foot on the table. It had the ankle tracker on it. "They might as well have left the handcuffs on. Ridiculous."

Sid downloaded the application Cyrus had sent her. A minute later, Smoke's location was on the screen. She showed it to him. "Works great. Things are looking up. Now, let's discuss our current situation... First, whatever you have in mind, you run by me first. Second, you don't go anywhere without me."

"I need to hit the head."

"Third." She looked at his boot on the table. "Keep it professional."

He dropped his foot on the floor.

"All right, but I really do."

"Make it quick."

He got up. "I missed prison chow this morning too." He patted his stomach. "I'd really like to have some pancakes."

She looked at him. "I don't care."

He picked up his duffle bag.

"Where are you going with that?"

"If you don't mind, I'm going to shave." He rubbed his chin. "This scruff makes me feel dirty. Now that I'm out of prison, I want to feel clean again."

"That really doesn't matter to me."

Smoke walked away and flipped a hallway switch.

"No bulbs."

Sid heard him checking switches until he finally stopped and a door near the back of the house closed. She checked the monitor on her phone. *Good.* Inside the file were more pictures of Adam Vaughn. He wore plain clothes and kept a personal network of goons close by. Most of the footage wasn't the best, as it came from security cameras and the locations were erratic.

Different banks. Restaurants—some expensive, others dives. AV seemed to have friends in high and low places. She became engrossed. There were pictures of weapons caches. Unidentified men slaughtered. There were pages of documentation with the letters blacked out.

What good is this?

There was an envelope inside she'd overlooked. She opened it. A brief letter was typed out on bureau letterhead.

Agent Shaw,

Due to the unorthodox arrangement of this assignment, you will need to keep the following items under consideration.

John Smoke is a convicted criminal with special skills. Don't underestimate him.

You have eyes on him and we have eyes on him. Allow him free range. We'll let you know if he needs to be reeled in.

If any alien objects or circumstances or individuals are encountered, notify your superiors immediately.

Trust your instincts and good hunting,

The Bureau

"Who on earth wrote this?" She glanced at her phone. Smoke's beacon hadn't moved. "It can't be from the bureau."

It was a first: a cryptic, unprofessional, unsigned letter. It made her wonder if Cyrus or Jack were playing a joke on her. But the bureau stamp. The make of the paper. She'd seen it before. It was nothing short of top brass bonding. She shook her head.

I guess there's a first time for everything.

She put the letter back inside the envelope and slipped it into her bag. *'Allow him free range', it says.* She smirked. *He doesn't need to know that.*

There was a squeak from down the hall. The turn of a faucet. The faint sound of water echoing.

Are you kidding me? A shower? Really? I thought he was hungry.

She glanced at the tracker on her phone. Nothing had changed.

One by one, she entered the location coordinates into her phone. Ten minutes later she was done.

Sidney brushed her hair aside. "I need a map." Her belly groaned. "Someone needs another shake." She gathered all the items up and stuck them back in the file folder. Calling out, "Let's get this show on the road," she made her way down the hall and listened at the door. The shower was still running. She rapped her knuckles on it. "Hey."

No reply.

She checked her tracker, and it showed no changes. She knocked again.

Her fingertips started to tingle. She drew her gun and tested the door handle. Locked.

"John? John Smoke?"

No reply.

She stepped back and delivered a heavy kick. The hollow door burst open. The mirror was steamed up, and the ankle tracker lay resting on the back of the toilet. She picked it up.

Damn. How'd he do that?

46

CHAPTER 9

ANGRY, SIDNEY RIPPED THE SHOWER curtain back. Smoke was in there.

"Hey! Do you mind?"

"What! Do I mind?" She looked away and slung the ankle tracker at him. "Put that back on!"

"I didn't want to get it wet," he said, chuckling.

"It's waterproof, imbecile!" Sidney left the room. Her face was flushed red. *How in the world did he do that?* "Get dressed and get out here!"

"I'm coming," he said from inside the bathroom. "What's the matter, Agent Shaw? Did you think all of your plans had gone up in Smoke?"

How did he do that? She stormed down the hall. Paced back and forth. Smoke rattled her. Nothing ever rattled her—until this assignment. *Get it together, Sid. Get it together.*

A few minutes later, Smoke came out. He was drying his dark hair off with his towel.

"Sorry about that," he said. "I didn't mean to startle you."

"I kicked the door in. You didn't hear that?"

"I was singing," he said, screwing up his face, "I think. Sometimes I get really into it."

"I didn't hear any singing." She glanced down at his ankle. The ankle tracker was back. "Care to explain?"

"I have my secrets."

"Do you want pancakes, little boy?"

"Okay, I made some calls."

Her head tilted over. "How did you do that?"

"I borrowed one of those agents' phones. The one who got a piece of taser." He held it out. "He can have it back now."

She snatched it from his hand and slipped it in her bag. "Who did you call?"

"My crew."

"And they remotely disarmed the ankle tracker?"

"Sure. Not a problem. And this model isn't one of the best ones. As soon as I gave them a model number, they laughed. So, they looped the signal and I unsnapped it. Easy peasy."

"Are you testing me, Mister Smoke?"

"I'm just knocking some dust off, Agent Shaw. We're going up against something big, and I need to be sharp." He tossed the towel aside and came closer. "I could have just vanished, you know."

"True, but then I wouldn't buy you any pancakes."

"Mmm," Smoke said. "That's good." He stuffed in another forkful of buttermilk pancakes slathered in syrup. He was half through his second stack. "You really should try some."

"No thanks," Sidney said again. She took a sip of coffee. She hadn't been inside an IHOP since she was a teenager. "I'm fine."

Smoke shrugged and stuffed in another mouthful. Over the past hour he'd proven himself to be the most elusive garbage disposal she'd ever known. He was a bit of a chatterbox too, asking her bizarre question after question that she ignored and dodged until they arrived at their high-carb destination.

She checked messages on her phone. Text. Email. Her niece, Megan, had dropped her a quick text that said 'Hi' with a smile and a unicorn. It had been a while since she heard from her. Her sister, Allison, had issues.

"What's the matter?" Smoke said, gulping down his second Coke and motioning for the waitress.

"Nothing." She set down her phone. "Tell me about this crew of yours."

A waitress took away his glass. "I'll be right back, Hun."

"Thanks," he said. "Sure, my crew. Right. Well, not much to tell. Just two friends that help me track things down. They work the inside, and I work the outside."

"Do they have names?"

"Fat Sam and Guppy."

"And this Fat Sam and Guppy are the ones that helped you hack into FBI property."

He nodded and shoved more pancake in his mouth. "Mmm! I swear, this makes me feel like I haven't eaten in months. Prison food has no flavor to it. And we never get pancakes or waffles, either. Which do you prefer?"

"Neither." She straightened herself in her seat. "Are you about finished?"

"Huh? Well, no. This is a carb load. The protein load comes next." He eyed her and her plate of half-eaten bacon. "You look like someone who knows something about that."

"Are your friends criminals?"

Smoke sat up and leered down. "No. Why would you say that?"

"I need to know what I'm dealing with. 'Fat Sam and Guppy' doesn't tell me much of anything." She took another sip of coffee. "You have to admit, it sounds shady."

"'Fat Sam and Guppy' sounds shady to you?"

"Yeah."

He shook his head. "Well, they say perception is everything."

The waitress returned with his third Coke. "Anything else, hun?"

Smoke looked at Sidney.

She glanced at the windows. The rain was pouring down, and the chill in her bones had finally faded. She gave him a nod.

Smoke held up the menu and pointed.

"I want this and this."

"Anything else?"

"I'll let you know when I'm through."

The waitress brushed by him. "You do that."

"Sure," Sidney said. "You do that. So, you were talking about Sam and Guppy?"

"No, you were talking about them." He took a drink. "Listen, they are legit. No record."

"Which implies they haven't been caught."

"Sort of, Agent Shaw... or Sidney... or Sid—can I call you that?"

"Let's keep it professional."

"Ugh... Agent Shaw, how suspicious are you of this hunt? I mean, think about it. They don't want you in the office. That limits resources. Instead, they want you to tail me as I go on a hunt. And you said yourself they weren't following protocol. Doesn't that worry you?"

"A little, maybe."

"Good. You're honest. Frankly I'm a bit worried too. Not in a scared way, but in a 'I'm pretty sure I'm being manipulated' kind of way."

"Then why do it?"

"It's the Black Slate. Bad people are on that list, and I like the idea of putting them away. Say, mind if I take a look at that file now?"

"Can you handle it while you're eating?"

"I'm a multitasker," he said, taking another big bite of pancakes.

She opened her bag and handed over the file. Smoke rummaged through it, his dark eyes scanning the contents. He was an attractive man. Boyish, yet dark. She noted white scar lines on his hands. A broken finger that hadn't healed well.

"He's a swarthy-looking Spaniard."

"Why do you say he's a Spaniard?"

Smoke shrugged. "He has some interesting haunts, too. Ew, look at all these dead guys. That's not good. Why did you show me this while I was eating?" He stuffed the papers inside the envelope. "I'm going to need a copy of this."

"It's confidential."

"Really?" He laughed. "I don't think there *is* such a thing these days."

The waitress returned and set down two steaming omelets surrounded by hash browns, all on one plate.

"Aw, you put them on one plate. That was really sweet of you. Thanks, sugar."

The waitress pinched his cheek. "If you weren't my son's age, I'd take you home with me." She looked at Sidney. "You found yourself a good one here. Big eater. I like a man that lets you feed him."

"Uh, we're not..." Sidney started, but the waitress moved on.

"Are you a good cook?" Smoke said, sharpening his knife with his fork.

"I can make an omelet."

"Well that's better than the last girl I dated."

"This isn't a date."

"Easy, I'm just making conversation."

"Let's stay on point, Mister Smoke."

"You see, there you go again. Just call me Smoke."

She held her tongue. She wanted to call him something else, but didn't.

"Agent Shaw, let me tell you how I expect things to go. I need information and a couple of days. I want to go to my place. Sort through some things. When I'm ready to move, I'll let you know and... we go."

"That's not going to happen. We're going to go back to the house and plan things out. We only have two weeks to resolve this."

He tilted his head back and closed his eyes. "Ugh. This is why I work alone."

"And you'd still be working alone if you hadn't gotten carried away with your last job."

"Just two days, that's all I ask. You take some time and I take some time. After that, I'll fill you in and be more willing to cooperate. Please."

The letter did say to turn him loose, but she wanted to hang on. That was her nature. Her training. This scenario was the complete opposite of everything she'd been taught. It irked her.

"You can take the ankle tracker off. That's the biggest problem. Why did you show your cards on that one?"

"Perhaps I was showing off a little."

"Here's the deal. You stay in the house. I drop you off. I pick you up. If I show up and the ankle tracker is there but you aren't, it's over."

"I'll keep it on if you insist, but take a moment. Don't you see the problem this ankle tracker presents? It's a distraction for us, nothing more. It doesn't benefit either of us. It only benefits *them*."

"Them?"

"You know," he said, eyeballing around. "Them."

I actually understand his point. "I tell you what, Mister Smoke. You finish your meal, we go back to the house, lay out a plan, and we'll see how it goes. Easy peasy?"

He dug into his omelet. "Good enough for me."

Her phone buzzed. It was another text from her niece, Megan. Her heart stopped. The text read:

Sorry to bother you, but I haven't seen Mommy in three days. I'm scared. A frowning icon followed.

CHAPTER 10

"What's going on?" Smoke said.

Sidney pulled the sedan into the driveway of the house, put it in park, and looked at him.

"Here's the deal. You go inside. You don't leave."

"Come on," he said. "You've been frosty the entire ride. What's going on? I can help."

"Get your bag. Get out of the car. Get inside the house."

Nodding and raising his hands in surrender, Smoke reached into the back seat and grabbed his duffle bag. He popped the door open to the sound of pouring rain outside. "Let me come."

"I'll be back tonight. Just go."

Smoke stepped into the rain, shut the door, and dashed onto the covered porch.

Sidney didn't wait to see if he went inside. She hit the gas, squealed out of the driveway, and blasted the car through the rain.

"Dammit!"

She was torn. On the one hand, she hated to let Smoke out of her sight. On the other, she didn't want him in her personal business.

It took her an hour and a half to get to her sister's apartment, talking to Megan the entire ride. The nine-year-old was tough, but scared. Sidney wheeled into the apartment complex, which consisted of twenty three-story brick buildings, a pool, tennis courts, and a gym—all of which were long past their glory days.

She parked, headed up the grass to the screened patio of her sister's porch, and knocked on the metal frame of the screen door.

"Megan? It's me, Aunt Sid."

A cute little face peeked through the blinds, and its watery eyes brightened. Megan unlocked the door, flung it open, ran outside, and hugged Sidney.

Sidney picked her up and carried her inside.

"It's all right. It's going to be all right."

Using her foot, she closed the door behind her and sat down on the couch with Megan latched onto her. Sidney's heart burst in her chest.

Allison had better not be using again.

"All right, Megan, all right. You're safe. I'm here." She pushed Megan back and wiped the tears from her eyes. The little girl's long brown hair was braided back in a ponytail. Her face was sweet and innocent with freckles on her nose. "I'm going to take care of you."

"I-I was doing fine. I even made it to school the last two days, but the storm scared me. I thought Mommy would be home by now, but she isn't. Do you think she's mad at me?"

"No, no, no, of course not." Sidney took a breath. Megan was a capable little girl. She'd learned how to take care of herself when she was little. An independent little thing. "She probably got lost again."

"Will you find her, Aunt Sid?"

"I will." She hugged her niece again. "I will."

Her sister, Allison, was younger. She was a runaway. An addict. A mess. Sidney could never make heads or tails of her problems, but she always tried to protect her. No matter what, Allison stayed in trouble. It was heartbreaking and infuriating.

"Are you hungry?"

"No," Megan said, "I had some cereal."

"Do you want to go stay with Nanny and Grandpa?"

"Can't you just stay here with me?" Megan looked at her with sad eyes. "Until Mommy comes back?"

"I'll see what I can do, but I have to call Nanny and Grandpa first."

Megan shrugged. She looked adorable. Little blue jeans. A flowery pink-and-purple shirt. "They'll do."

Sidney didn't stick around after her mother arrived. Keeping the reunion short, she hit the road and headed to Allison's ex-boyfriend's... Dave was his name. According to Megan, he'd been coming around and staying over from time to time. The last time she'd seen Dave and Megan together, it hadn't ended well.

If she's with him, I might kill both of them.

She drove the car into another neighborhood a

little better than the one where she'd left Smoke. The sidewalks and driveways made up the edges of well-kept lawns. Leaves were in piles and bagged at the end of the drives. She pulled along the sidewalk across the street from Dave's house, 104 Dickers Street. The windows were barred. The screen door was a wrought-iron security door. The garage door was closed.

Somebody's made some changes since the last time I was here.

She checked her phone. Smoke's beacon remained in place.

He'd better be there.

The blinds were shut, but light peeked out at the corners. She waited. Dave was a dealer. A clever one. He moved small quantities to subsidize his government assistance. He hadn't worked in years—or ever, for all she knew. She waited another hour. Cars splashed by. Water poured into the grates. It was 2:15 p.m. when she looked again. She needed to get back to Smoke. She needed to find her sister.

I need to put an ankle tracker on her!

She drummed her fingernails on the steering wheel. Chewed on her lip.

Aw, screw it.

She popped the trunk, opened her door, and stepped out into the rain. From the trunk she grabbed an umbrella and opened it up. A car rolled by, splashed her legs, and pulled into Dave's driveway. She noted the plate.

A couple of young men in hoodies jumped out of the car and rushed onto the stoop. One started pounding on the door. The other was yelling.

"Hurry up! It's cold as hell out here!"

The door opened. Sidney hid behind the umbrella until she heard the door close, then made her way across the street and waited beside the front door on the stoop, craning her neck toward the window. The voices were muffled, and the driving rain splattering all around drowned out the details. She closed the umbrella, shook it off, and waited. Ten minutes later, the door opened. She stepped back and whipped out her badge.

The dilated eyes of the young men lifted toward her.

Sidney held her badge up and said quietly, "Disappear."

The two scurried through the rain without a glance backward.

Sidney caught the door with her umbrella and slipped inside.

"Shut the door, you idiots!" a voice said. Dave appeared in the foyer. His eyes widened. He dropped his can of beer. "Aw shit! How'd you get in here?"

Sidney closed the door behind her and locked it.

"Hey, hey," Dave said, holding his hands up and backing away into the living room. "I didn't do anything."

"Sure you didn't, Dave. Sure."

Dave wasn't a bad-looking guy. He had a mop of brown hair and strong features. A scruffy beard. The plaid pajama pants and Bob Marley T-shirt did little to enhance his demeanor. His eyes were weak and yellow, and he smelled like reefer.

"You can't be in here," he said. "It's illegal."

"Where is Allison, Dave?"

His eyes flitted around the room. A bong sat on the

coffee table in front of a new plush sectional sofa. A video game was playing on a seventy-inch flat-screen TV.

"I haven't seen her."

"Do you remember what happened the last time you lied to me about her?"

Grimacing, he rubbed the white scar on his forehead. "Yes."

Sidney got closer and bounced the handle of the umbrella on his shoulder.

"Don't make me use this."

"What are you going to do with an umbrella?" He laughed. "Let me guess. Stick it where the sun don't shine and open it?"

"Aw, that's my darling Dave. Smart-ass dope head and everything." She stepped on his toe. "You know what, Dave? I really like your idea."

"You would, seeing how you don't have any of your own." He tugged his foot out. "And as I recall, you got into quite a bit of trouble the last time you barged in here, didn't you?"

"Oh, you gonna call your uncle again, the congressman?"

"Yep."

"Hmmm," she said, tapping the umbrella on his shoulder. "I think he's in danger of losing this next election. Yes, I'm pretty sure he's done for."

"No he isn't. He's up in the polls."

She smiled.

"I'll take my chances."

She brought the umbrella handle down between his eyes.

Crack!

"Ow! You bitch!"

Crack!

"Ugh! Stop it!"

"Stop it what?"

"Sid!"

Crack!

"Agent Shaw! Okay? Agent Shaw!"

"Dave, this is the last time that I ask. Where is she?"

He swallowed hard and looked away.

Sidney made it over to the coffee table, picked up the bong, and started to pour the water out on his new couch.

"Be nice, now. I didn't do this. I swear it's not my fault."

"Where IS she?"

"I-I…"

Sidney dropped some more water on the sofa.

"Aw…" Dave moaned.

"If you like, Dave, I'll be more than happy to confiscate your inventory."

"Not without a warrant."

She poured out the bong and dropped it on the couch.

"Dammit, that's new!"

She took out her phone.

"I'm out of patience. One call, and a swarm of local law enforcement will be here."

"You wouldn't dare. Not after the last time."

She started to dial.

Dave turned tail and ran up the steps.

"Allison! Allison! Run!"

Sidney surged up the stairs and stormed down the hallway just as Dave jetted into a bedroom and slammed the door behind him.

Sidney pounded on the door.

"Open up! I'm not playing any games! Get out of there, Allison!"

"Screw you, *Agent* Shaw!" Dave yelled.

She kicked the door in.

Dave stood inside an unkempt bedroom with the window wide open. One leg hung outside the sill.

She grabbed him by the arm, jerked him inside, and wrestled him to the floor.

"No more games, Dave."

"You're too late," he said, laughing. "She's already gone."

She checked outside the window. There was a deck and stairs that led down into the backyard. There was no sign of Allison.

"She left you a message, Sid," Dave said, sitting up and rubbing his head.

"Really, what was that?"

He giggled. "You are so stupid."

"Am I? Why is that?"

She heard the rumble of a garage door opening.

"Because," Dave said, "she was never up here to begin with. It was all a distraction, you stupid b—"

She socked him in the jaw, rocking his head back to the carpet. *Whap!* She dashed downstairs and opened the front door. A jungle-green Jeep Wrangler sped out of the garage down the street and disappeared around the corner.

"Damn!"

CHAPTER 11

S IDNEY RUSHED TO HER CAR and slung open the door. Taking a seat, she glanced back at Dave's house. A blind in one of the top bedrooms peeked open. She saw the faint outline of two fingers.

Wait a minute.

She took a second and closed her eyes, envisioned the Jeep Wrangler speeding away. There was a lone driver hunched over the wheel. Big. Husky. Allison could have been hidden in the back seat. Or maybe not. She had a feeling. An instinct.

That little dope-headed witch is still in there.

The garage door started to close.

Crap! Move it, Sid!

She couldn't let Dave lock her out again. And she dared not force herself in, not after the last time. She was probably in enough trouble already. She sprinted across the street, right in front of an oncoming car. It squealed to a stop, and the driver laid on the horn. She kept moving, eyes intent on the lowering garage door.

She wasn't going to make it. She made a decision and did a stupid thing.

Sidney drew her gun and slung it under the garage door. It skidded over the driveway, clearing the opening by inches and disappearing inside. The door stopped, rattled... and began to lift. She heard a voice inside scream. Up the door went. One foot. Two feet. It stopped and renewed its descent. Sidney rolled underneath it and inside. She spied her gun, scrambled to it, and found Dave's wide eyes.

"No!" he said, making his way back inside through the door. "No! Get out of here!"

Sidney snatched up her weapon and charged the closing door that was slamming shut. She lowered her shoulder and plowed into it. The impact jarred the door open. It jarred Dave.

"You get out of here! This is illegal!"

She drove her knee into his crotch. She shoved him inside the garage and watched him spill onto the floor, cry out, and writhe. She slammed the door shut and locked it.

Upstairs, she heard footfalls scampering over the floor. There was something about them—lithe, child-like, familiar. She made it upstairs in seconds. A woman with long dark hair, blue jeans, and a black T-shirt ambled across the hall into another room and stumbled inside the door.

"Allison!"

Two bare feet slipped into the frame, and the bedroom door started to close. Sidney stopped it with her foot and shoved it open. She looked down at her sister. Allison was a smaller version of herself, but soft and supple. She was shaking. Her face was sad. Tears streamed out of her eyes. There were needle tracks on one arm.

"I'm sorry, Sid. I'm sorry."

"Shut up," Sidney said. "Do you know how long it's been since you left Megan?"

"A day?" Allison sniffed.

"Three days!"

"No," Allison said, shaking her head. "It, it can't have been."

"Well, it has."

Allison started to bawl. Tears streamed out of her sunken eyes and over her pouting lips. "I'm a lousy mother."

"You're a lousy sister too. Get up!"

"What? Why? I'm not leaving. I don't deserve to go back."

Sidney reached down and grabbed her arm.

"Get up!"

Allison jerked away. "No!"

Here we go. Her little claws are coming out.

"I'll take you out of here in handcuffs."

Allison pounced on her legs and drove her to the floor. Sidney cracked her head on the door frame, drawing spots in her eyes.

"No you won't!" Allison screamed. She sprang out of the door.

Angry, Sidney snatched her sister's ankle and climbed onto her back.

"Get off me! Get off me! Dave!"

Sidney wrenched Allison's arms behind her back. Her

sister squealed. She bound up her wrists and slipped the flexi-cuffs on her. Allison resumed her bawling.

"Get up. I'm not carrying you."

"No," Allison said with a defiant sob. "No."

She grabbed Allison by the ankles and started dragging her toward the stairs. Her sister kicked at her and yelled.

"I hate you! I hate you, Sid! I hate you! Why can't you mind your own business? Why can't you leave me alone!"

This wasn't the first time the sisters had gone round and round. It all started in their teens. Allison liked to party. She liked the attention. She liked boys. Drugs. Excitement. Sidney bailed her little sister out time and again. It got old. It had made her mom and dad old.

"Why don't you grow up, you little brat! You have a daughter. Go to church and find Jesus or something." She hauled Allison down the carpeted stairs.

"Hey!"

"Get up, then!"

At the landing, Allison started to rise. She eyeballed Sidney. She spat in her face.

Sidney slapped her across the jaw, and Allison stumbled back to the floor. Her little sister wailed. "I hate you, Sid. I hate you."

Sidney dragged her to her feet and said, "You don't hate me. You hate yourself."

Family. It mattered, even though her sister was a wild one who often ruined the best-planned Thanksgiving. Sidney loved her sister, even though for the last decade she'd wanted to choke her. And there was Megan. How could Allison neglect Megan? The little beauty was about one step from a foster home if she and their parents didn't intervene.

Please God. Please don't let that happen.

Sidney pulled into a gas station alongside the pumps. It was evening now, and she'd just spent the last three hours helping her parents get Allison settled down. They were all distraught, and none more so than Allison had been when she was finally reunited with Megan. She had shaken all over and sobbed, begging forgiveness. All Megan had said was, "It's going to be okay, Mommy."

Megan was a strong little lady.

Sidney whipped out her credit card, pumped gas, ran inside the station, and grabbed some coffee. Black. No cream. No sugar. No straws. She dropped two bucks on the counter and left, ignoring the greasy-haired clerk's toothy smile at her.

Creep.

She racked the nozzle, grabbed her receipt, and hopped back inside the car to lean back against the headrest and take a long sigh.

Lousy weather. Lousy day. I should have transferred south when I had the chance. What was I thinking?

Family. She rubbed the knot on the side of her head.

Love hurts.

She took a sip of coffee and checked her phone. Smoke's location hadn't changed.

He'd better be there—probably wants more pancakes.

She put the car in drive, sped out onto the main

drag, and gunned it onto the highway. Her thoughts were riddled with her family. The burden on Mom and Dad. Dealing with Allison's problems. And Megan. This was one of the things she hated about her job. She loved her duty. She loved her family. But duty presided over family, and it hurt in times like this when they needed her.

"It's all right," her mother, Sally, had assured her. "We understand. It's our job to handle this. We'll get her on the mend."

Her father, Keith, had agreed and nodded his head. Both of her parents were strong, but they were heartbroken, and they weren't getting any younger. She could see it in their eyes. She heard the worry in their voices, not just for Allison, but for her. They didn't like the job she did. It was dangerous. And oftentimes Sidney felt selfish. It tore at her.

Block it out. Block it out, Sid. You can't take care of everybody.

Sidney had to live her life and be available when she could.

"Just do the best you can, Sid," her father had said, giving her one last hug. His hugs were always warm and comforting. "Do the best you can."

I try, but it never feels like enough.

CHAPTER 12

IT WAS 8:14 P.M. WHEN she pulled into the driveway of the FBI house. Smoke's beacon was still strong, but the porch lights were out, and so was the lamppost at the end of the drive.

He's not here. I know it.

The front door was locked, and none of the inside lights shone. She took out the house key that Jack had given her and fumbled around with the lock until she got it. Inside she went, testing the switches until she made it to the lamp between the living room and kitchen and switched it on.

With caution she made her way down the hallway. A dim light showed beneath one of the doors. She put her ear to it and heard voices on the other side. She drew her weapon, turned the knob, and opened the door. A set of wooden stairs led into a basement she hadn't accounted for. Weapon first, she crept down them.

The basement was partially finished. There were hook-ups for laundry and an unfinished shower. The framework of two-by-four walls was laid out. There was an empty fireplace and a rec room or den of some sort. A flat-screen TV was on. In front of it was a plaid sofa, and there was an old recliner that didn't match beside it. A news show was on the screen. A lady doing the weather.

What is going on here?

She noticed a wooden kitchen table with some papers fanned out on it. A pizza box and a two-liter of soda. Some power tools and drywall were lying nearby on the floor. There was a map hanging on a plywood wall.

A commode flushed.

Sidney whirled around.

Smoke stepped out from behind a narrow bathroom door. He lifted his hands up.

"Easy, Shooter. I'm just taking a ten-fourteen, is all." He eyed the gun and cocked a feeble smile. "Glad you're back. Is everything okay? You look like you've had a long day."

She holstered her weapon.

"What is going on here?" She glided back to the table and took a closer look at the contents. The file folder was on the table. Her blood pressure spiked. "You stole my file."

Hands still up, Smoke said, "I can explain."

"Can you now?"

"Sure, I, er... okay, I stole it, but only so that I could work on things while you were gone." He walked over to his map and pointed at the red circles. "See, now we can take another angle on things."

"You made a mistake."

"I'm sorry," he said, "but I stayed put. I bet you thought I wouldn't, didn't you?"

Her stomach gurgled.

Smoke opened the pizza box. "Half ham and onions and half Hawaiian. Please, have some."

"How did you get this?"

"Uh… Delivery."

"And how did you pay for it? Did you spend my money too?"

"No," he said, "I'd never do that." He tapped his head. "I have many numbers in my head. Hey, my accounts are still good."

"Well, you did one thing right today."

"I did? What's that?"

Sidney picked up a slice of pizza and took a seat on the sofa.

"I like Hawaiian."

The old sofa was comfortable. It reminded her of the times she and Allison would stay in their grandparents' basement for long weekends. She bit into the pizza.

"I could warm it up," Smoke said. "I came down here and saw that some of the breakers were off, but I let them be. I didn't want any nosy neighbors dropping by for a greeting. I like my privacy."

Sidney yawned. An image of Megan came to mind, and she forced it out again. She studied the television. "So, you're getting reception down here."

"I spliced into the box."

"Cable theft is a crime," she said with a laugh.

Smoke eased into the recliner.

"So, I'm here. You're here. What's the next move?"

I have no idea.

"You look beat," he continued.

"I look beat? Really?"

"Sorry, I guess *tired* is a better word."

She finished off the pizza and dusted off her hands. She wanted to lie down, but she forced herself off the sofa instead and headed toward the map.

"Where did you get the map? Did the pizza guy deliver that too?"

"Er... well, you shouldn't be surprised at what you can get delivered these days. As a matter of fact, Amazon—"

"Save it. I don't care to know." She eyed the map that was tacked to the wall. Smoke had seven locations circled and named in colored Sharpie. "I guess they delivered the thumb tacks and pens, too." She faced him. He sat with an innocent look on his face. "Is there anything else you care to share that you *ordered*? Should I expect a delivery from QVC?"

"No."

Her thoughts raced.

He could have had a gun delivered. Anything! "Get up!"

"What?"

"I said, 'get up'!"

"But—"

She drew her gun. "Now!"

Slowly he came out of the chair.

"Put your hands on your head."

"Okay."

She held her weapon barrel up under his neck, kept her eyes on him, and patted him down. Her fingers found a gun tucked in the back of his pants.

"Sit."

Smoke obeyed.

"Where did you get this?"

"From the same agent that I got the handcuff keys from. Smith & Wesson .45 ACP." He smiled. "A fine weapon. But he doesn't deserve it if he can't secure it."

"And you don't deserve it either."

"You can't expect me to traverse troubled waters without a weapon in hand."

"No one said anything about you getting a weapon. It's illegal for a convict to possess one."

"I'm not a—oh, never mind." He flopped back into his seat. "Fine. Keep it."

She stuffed it in the back of her pants.

"Thank you."

How did he steal a weapon from an agent? She turned and faced the map again, hiding the grin on her face. *Impressive. I wish I could see Jack's face when he finds out.*

"So tell me, Mister Smoke, what have you learned from all of these locations?"

"Smoke, and they have nothing of use whatsoever."

"What do you mean? There has to be something here."

He got up and picked up the pictures from the table. "All of these pictures of Adam Vaughn at all of these locations. Well, guess what."

"Humor me?"

"These photos are doctored."

CHAPTER 13

S IDNEY STUDIED THE PHOTOS.

"You have to be kidding me."

"I wish I was," Smoke said.

She took a seat at the kitchen table and eyed each photo one by one. Smoke was right. The shadows were bad. The angles off. Faint white lines showed where images had been trimmed and cropped. Repetition of pixels. A lack of reflections. They were good fakes, really good. She'd spent months working with the FBI's digital forensics labs. She should have caught this right off the bat. She pushed her hair back from her eyes.

I'm an idiot.

Ever since Jack woke her up, her entire day had been rush, rush, rush. Everything was off beat. Unorthodox. She liked order. She liked a plan. She liked to be in charge.

Today is not my day.

"You have a good eye," she said. "I have to admit I'm surprised. And I hate to admit that I missed it."

"You hardly looked at them." He cleared his throat. "Given the evidence, I have a suggestion."

Sidney sifted through the file. There were rap sheets on some of the faces that accompanied Adam Vaughn.

"We'll go after them," she said.

"We?"

"Sure. You're used to stakeouts, aren't you?"

"Not with a partner. And I thought I was going this alone and reporting back to you."

"Given the circumstances, I think it's best that we stay together. I feel more comfortable keeping an eye on things."

Smoke scratched his forehead. "So, when do we start this stakeout?"

"When I say so."

The couch groaned when Smoke lay down. "Great, wake me up when you're ready to go."

Sidney continued her closer inspection of the papers in the file. Pictures. Names. Places. Drug labs. Murder scenes. Illegal arms. Adam Vaughn was in a mish-mash of illegal behavior.

"You know," Smoke said, "I'm sure you know we're being set up to fail. Or at least I am."

"I thought you were taking a nap."

"No, I was just thinking. Honestly, Agent Shaw, just let me go at this alone. There's no reason you need to get hurt."

She began organizing the papers and pictures in neat little piles.

"I beg your pardon?"

"Think about it, The Black Slate, it's just a ruse.

They don't really want us to find those criminals. Or at least not AV. They just want paperwork for the files so that it looks like they're trying to put them down. It's all baloney."

Oh Lord, that's exactly what I was thinking ... Quick, find a reason to not like this guy.

"Sounds like you read a lot of conspiracy books in prison." She plucked out the picture of a beefy dog-faced man named Rod Brown. "Do you lose a lot of sleep over it?"

"I always sleep like a baby."

"Except now, unfortunately."

"You really don't have to be so defensive," he said. We're on the same team, remember?"

"We aren't a team."

"Then what are we?"

She found his eyes. "Screwed." She held up the picture of Rod Brown. "But not as bad as this guy when we find him."

"So this is your plan, stake out this Rod Brown fella?" Smoke sat in the passenger seat with a frown on his face. "With a face like that, he must have had a hard life. He looks like a bulldog. Maybe a Rottweiler. Why'd you pick him?"

"He looks stupid."

"Man, why didn't I think of that? Wow, you really learn great things at the academy." He fanned the photo. "Just shake down the stupid-looking people."

Sidney wanted to laugh, but she didn't. It was difficult because she liked joking around. She often did with the people she worked with once she got to know them. Yawning, she focused on the road.

"You'll be sharper if you get some rest," Smoke suggested. "Tell you what. How about you let me drive this racing machine. Crown Vic. Rear wheel drive. Small block V-8. Pretty slow muscle if you ask me, but I can make it fun." He toyed with the dash. "What year is this thing? Two thousand eight?"

"Nine."

"Oh. Seems older. How about I put some music on. What kind do you like?"

She could feel his eyes on her. "How about you leave it alone."

"I bet you like talk radio."

"No, what I like is *no talking about the radio.*"

Smoke blanched. "Wow. That was almost funny." Smoke leaned back in his seat and perused the file. "So are we going to Mister Brown's apartment or hangout? I'd try the apartment first. It's too early for the hangout. What do you think?"

"I think you'll know when we get there."

"That isn't exactly fair," he said. "I need a little time to visualize and prepare. You know, a heads up."

Sidney laid down the accelerator and zoomed up the interstate's passing lane. She loved the feeling of the car pushing forward.

"You're breaking the speed limit," Smoke said. "Huh, I bet you're one of those speed demons. Where did you say you were from? Bristol?"

He's annoying. Perhaps I should let him work alone.

Smoke kept talking and she continued her silence. Too many things were running through her mind. The doctored pictures were a problem. Surely someone else had studied them, Jack perhaps. The digital forensics lab. Who had made them? Why the deception? She had been with the FBI five years, and until today, the job had been cut and dried. And that begged another question. Why her? And why had her old boss, Ted, recommended extraordinary caution?

"So, how's your family?" Smoke said.

"Great."

He bobbed his head. "That's good to hear. Do they live in the area?"

"No."

"Well, not the immediate area, but maybe within a few counties or so? You sound local. Very, very local."

"A lot of people say that about me."

"A lot of people such as... friends?"

I'm going to shoot him.

"I noticed a little indentation on your ring finger," Smoke continued. "Are you divorced? It's funny how that ring seems permanent. It wasn't Cyrus, was it?" Smoke pulled down his visor and checked his hair in the mirror. "No, it's been a while since you two had your thing. But I have to say, you and Cyrus... you have to admit that was a huge mismatch."

"Shut up."

"Fine." Smoke zipped his mouth shut, locked it, powered down the window, and tossed out the imaginary key. He closed the window and held out his hands.

And this guy used to be a Navy SEAL? Geez.

She blocked Smoke's humming out until they arrived at Rod Brown's condominium and parked on the street just outside the parking lot. The record didn't state whether he drove a car or not. She checked the address in the file. Unit 12, room 11. She checked her watch. 10:35 p.m.

"If you stop humming, I'll let you listen to the radio while we wait."

Smoke mumbled from behind his sealed lips.

"Enough, please," she said.

"So, now what? We're just going to sit here?"

"Yep."

"Uh... and what if he's on vacation or out on the job?"

She shrugged. "We'll see."

Smoked stared out his window. "Why don't you let me go and see if he's in his condo?"

"No."

"Come on. Just give me a little bit of leash. It's not like I haven't ever performed recon before. Please."

His words softened her. She didn't like it. "Ten minutes—"

Smoke popped open the door.

"Stop right there!"

He shut the door in her face and disappeared between the buildings.

Sidney closed her hanging jaw.

I'll give him ten minutes. If he's not back by then, I'm going to catch him and kill him. She pounded her fist on the dash. *Men!*

She took out her phone. Smoke's beacon remained in the area. A text message popped up from her mother.

"It's going to be a long few nights, but we'll be fine. Jeff is here. Don't worry."

Jeff was a lifelong friend who had handled Allison before. A good guy. Calm under pressure.

Sidney didn't respond. If she did, her mother would keep texting all night.

I'll check tomorrow.

She checked the time. 10:41 p.m. Smoke's beacon was unmoving.

Maybe this is a good thing. Let go, Sid. Let go. You can't control everybody. Just like you can't control Allison.

She drummed her fingers on the steering wheel. The car was fogging up, so she rolled down the window. There were more than a dozen buildings in the complex. Rod's was one away from the highway. His place was on the first floor. The file said he was a very husky guy, three hundred pounds or so.

Sidney reached into the back seat and dug a pair of binoculars out of a gym bag. She spied on the sidewalk that led in front of the condo. It was dark, but the lamp posts gave off a dim light in the steady rain.

10:44.

One more minute and it's go time.

She kept the binoculars up. A hulking figure stepped into view.

What in the...

Smoke was running straight for her with a large man hefted over his shoulder.

He's insane!

CHAPTER 14

"**O**PEN THE DOOR! OPEN THE door!" Smoke yelled.

Sidney popped the locks.

Smoke swung open the back door and stuffed the hefty body inside. The back sagged and bounced with the impact. Smoke shoved the man over, hopped in the back seat with him, and shut the door.

"What are you doing? Have you gone mad?"

"Did I make it?" Smoke asked, scanning the dash.

"Make what?"

"Make it back in ten minutes?"

"Are you kidding me?"

"No, you said ten minutes. I made it, didn't I?" He pumped his fist. "Yes, one of my best extractions ever!"

Sidney stared at the man in the back seat. It was Rod Brown. A white cotton tank-top barely contained his belly. His plaid boxer shorts were half turned around. He was out. Out cold.

"Go," Smoke said. "Go! I think someone might have seen me."

"No."

"Yes!" Smoke said. "I see someone coming."

A flashlight coming from the condos cut through the dank night.

Sidney dropped the transmission into drive and sped away. "Do you know how many laws you've broken?"

"Let's see…" He counted on his fingers. "Breaking and entering, and kidnapping. Two."

"Two to start with."

Rod Brown groaned.

Smoke socked him in the jaw. *Whap!* "And battery."

"You're an idiot!"

"Look," Smoke said, "the way I see it, he's a criminal."

"So are you."

"No—aw, let's not get into that. That said, guys like him don't operate within the rules you hold so dear. They break them. And we aren't going to get anywhere following the FBI playbook." Smoke huffed. "Guys like this laugh at those tactics. If you want to get this done, then we need to fight fire with fire."

"We need to not break the law."

"Then you shouldn't have come along, Agent Shaw. I'm pretty sure that's the reason they hired me to do this: I can get my hands dirty. You can't." He shoved Rod's sagging body over toward the window. "Let me out, and you walk away from this."

"No." In the rearview mirror, she saw Smoke banging his head against his headrest.

I'm in charge, not you.

"So what's the next step in your brilliant plan? Are we going to beat the whereabouts of AV out of him?" she asked.

"Something like that, but my methods of intimidation are a bit more subtle."

"Waterboarding?"

Smoke laughed. "Sure. Why not? Let's swing by Walmart and pick up some bottled water and towels."

Sidney drove the car down into a marina along the Potomac and parked in the shadows where a stretch of highway passed over. She turned and faced Smoke. "Next time, let's put him in the trunk."

"Next time, huh?"

"You know what I mean."

"Sure. Say, where are your flex cuffs?"

She popped open the glove box and handed him two pairs.

Smoke fastened Rod's arms behind his back and bound his ankles. He rummaged through Sidney's gym bag.

"Hey!" She snatched a pair of her panties from his hand. "Do you mind?"

"No," Smoke said. He found a sweatshirt and covered Rod's head. "There. I think we're ready to go now." He handed over her gym bag. "All set. Time to wake him up." He put his finger to his lips. "Let me do the talking."

"Fine. Just don't get carried away." Interrogations. She'd conducted plenty. *Let's see how you handle this.*

"Great, now turn the heater up."

She did.

Smoke nodded. "And cover your ears."

"Why?"

Smoke pinched Rod's inner thigh.

The big man bucked in his seat and let out an ear-splitting howl.

Sidney covered her ears.

Smoke grabbed Rod by his neck and squeezed. "Quiet, Rod, and we'll make this quick."

"Who-who are you?" Rod stammered. "What's going on?"

"I just have a few questions." Smoke changed his voice to something, rougher, darker. "Tell me what I need to know, and I'll let you go."

"Screw you! Do you know who I am?"

"You're Rod Brown. Another one of AV's disposable buttholes."

"Huh? What did you call me? A disposable—"

Smoke punched his face through the sweatshirt. "Shut up!"

"But—"

Punch!

"I don't like your accent. Where are you from, Rod? Pennsylvania? Jersey?"

"Baltimore."

Punch!

"I thought I told you to keep quiet. And I hate Baltimore." Smoke winked at Sidney. "Now, simple question. Where can I find AV?"

Rod remained still and silent. The rising heat was fogging up the windows. Sidney fanned her neck.

"I asked you a question, Rod."

Rod said nothing.

"Oh, I see. Now you're going to be quiet."

Punch.

"Listen, moron," Rod said. "You can punch me all you want, but I don't know any AV."

"Sure, sure you don't. And I'm Mary Poppins."

"You sound like her to me, you frigging putz!" Rod thrashed at his bonds. "Now let me out of these things, you idiot, and I won't have to frigging kill you!"

Smoke reached under the sweatshirt, hooked his fingers into Rod's nose, and lifted him up out of his seat. It was one of Sidney's favorite pressure points. A simple restraining technique. *Impressive.*

"Ow! Ow! Ow!"

"Do you know who AV is, or don't you?"

"Yes! Yes!"

"Are you going to sit still?"

"Yes! Ow! Yes!"

Smoke released him.

"Good, Baltimore Rod. Now we're getting somewhere. So tell me—you're one of his crew—where is he?"

"Look," Rod said, huffing for breath, "Let me do both of us a favor. Whatever you have with AV, drop it. If you pursue it, then you're dead already."

"So you know where he is?"

"All I know is when and where I'm supposed to be. He may or may not be there. Listen, whoever you are, I don't care." Rod's voice started to break. He balled up a little. "Don't cross AV. Don't make me cross AV. It's worse than death, what he does to people who cross him. Worse than death."

An uncanny chill raced down Sidney's spine. She glanced at Smoke. One of his brows was cocked over his eye. He mouthed some words to her. "What do you make of that?"

She shrugged.

84

He held a finger up, reached into his pocket and handed her a smartphone. He nodded to Rod.

Sidney turned it on. It needed a passcode. *Great.* She thought about it as Smoke went back to work.

"When's your next meeting with AV?"

"Two days."

"Oh, that was pretty quick. I think you're lying, Baltimore Rod." Smoke lightly touched his fingers on Rod's leg.

"Eek! What was that?"

"A spider. Well, a tarantula to be exact." He tickled Rod's leg again.

Rod screamed. "Get it off me! Please! Get it off me!"

"What's the matter, Rod? Are you scared of a little, er, well, a big bug with eight hairy legs?" He barely touched the hair on Rod's leg again.

"Ah!" The big man bucked and twitched. "Stop it! I meet him tomorrow. Late afternoon! Stop it!"

"Where?"

Rod fell silent.

"My spider is a biter, Rod."

"Please, man, please. You don't want to do this. If I tell you, AV will figure it out. AV knows everything. No one can get close to him, no matter how hard they try. Trust me, man. Trust me!" He sobbed. "It's a death wish."

Sidney had seen plenty of men under duress before, but she hadn't expected this. Given enough pressure, loyal foot soldiers rolled on their bosses all the time. This was different. Rod had fear. Real, earnest fear.

Hmmm... She decided to try a passcode on Rod's

phone. *Let's see how dumb you are.* She typed in his building and room number. 1211. She got access. *Yes!* She showed Smoke. His brows lifted. She began sifting through Rod's emails, contacts, texts, and interesting applications. It was sparse. *Great. A burner.*

"Where are you meeting tomorrow?" Smoke said.

"Aw geez, don't make me, please."

"I'm going to leave you in here with Mister Tarantula. Leave him on your face. How does that sound, Rod?" Smoke tickled his leg.

"Ah! No! No!"

"Ah, yes, yes," Smoke said.

"It's Drake. A club called Drake. He meets us there. Oh man. Oh man, I can't believe I told you." He balled up and started to rock. "I'm a dead man. You're a dead man. All loose ends must go."

CHAPTER 15

Smoke put Rod in a sleeper hold and silenced the man's hysteria. "Sorry," he said, "that was getting old."

"Agreed." Sidney tossed the phone back to Smoke. "So what's the plan now? Are you going to tuck him back in bed?"

"We could drug him."

"I don't have any drugs. Do you?"

"I was thinking we could buy some."

"Dumb idea. I guess you didn't think things through." Sidney fastened her belt and put the car in drive. In two minutes they were back on the highway.

This is a mess. A total mess.

"You did good," Smoke said.

"I beg your pardon?"

"You did good. You have good instincts. Going after Baltimore Rod was a good call. He *is* stupid, and he was easy to break."

"I think some luck should be factored in there, seeing as he was home. What if he hadn't been?"

"Well, he was though, wasn't he?"

Sidney fought off a yawn.

"Tired?"

She ignored him. Exhausted was more like it. It had been an unexpectedly emotional day, and she hadn't handled it well. *I need to get better at this.*

"I think we should follow your suggestion and tuck Baltimore Rod back in bed."

Sidney caught Smoke's eyes in the rearview mirror. "Why is that?"

"Why do you think? You suggested it."

"You first."

"Aw, can you just be forthcoming for once and let me be the devil's advocate for a change?"

"All right, Mister Smoke, let me share my thoughts. You're an idiot! All you had to do was verify that Rod was in there. We could have tailed him. Bugged him. Done something vastly more subtle."

"That might have taken days. Maybe weeks."

"And after a few days we could have improvised," she said.

"I improvised early. Now we know where AV will be."

"Might be. And that's assuming Rod isn't lying."

"He's not."

"Why, because you pretended to put a spider on his leg?"

"You have to admit, it was pretty effective, one of my better ones." He leaned forward. "It's called entomophobia. People that are raised in the city are twice as likely to get big heebie-jeebies as folks in the country. It pays off for me most times."

"Luck."

"Fate," he said.

"Well, I think the mentioning of AV shook him," she said, hitting the car's blinker and switching lanes. "And to your point, I think that gives us an advantage. He won't tell AV. That would be bad for him too. You can just put him back in his apartment. He's so scared of AV that I'm betting he'd rather hide his secret than go on the run. It at least gives him a pleading chance."

Smoke eased into his seat. "My thoughts exactly, Agent Shaw. Well done."

"Shut up."

It was 12:42 am when they got back to the FBI house. Baltimore Rod was back in his condo asleep—with the help of some Sominex Smoke had forced down his throat.

"He'll sleep like a baby," Smoke said. "He might even forget the whole thing."

I'd like to forget this whole thing.

Sidney sat on the basement couch while Smoke started up the gas fireplace in the corner. The warm light was soothing. Too soothing. She yawned again.

"If you're going to stay over," Smoke said, taking a place on the recliner, "you might as well catch some *z*'s."

Sidney sat up and toggled through her phone. She'd downloaded all of Baltimore Rod's information from his burner before she returned it. There were a few nuggets that were useful. Times. Locations. A month's worth of data. It was a stroke of luck that he hadn't pitched it by now. She covered her mouth and yawned.

I need sleep. I need to be sharp tomorrow.

She was heading into a twenty-four-hour day, and it had been a while. At least a year. She'd gotten used to six hours of sleep during the week—eight on the weekends. In the Air Force, when she was law enforcement, there had been days that lasted forty-eight to seventy-two hours. There were long stake-outs with the FBI, but they weren't so bad.

I've gotten soft.

She rubbed her blurry eyes and took a glance at Smoke. He sat rubbing the grizzle on his chin, with the fire's flame reflecting in his dark eyes.

Well, look at Mister Bright-eyed and Bushy-tailed.

"This reminds me of my grandmother's place," he said. "She had a basement I'd stay in whenever Mom and Dad took trips out of town." He started to rock a little in the recliner. "It was so easy to start a fire with a gas line built in. I'd play with the flames all night. Huddle in front of the TV and play Nintendo. And Nanny, she fed us hot chocolate with ice cream."

Sidney rose up off the sofa. "I'll see you in the morning."

"You're leaving? Why?"

"Because you're ruining my image of the Navy SEALs."

"Because I like Nintendo?"

"No, because I don't want to know what your favorite ice cream is."

"It's—"

"See you tomorrow," she said, heading up the steps.

"What time?"

"Morning time." She stopped at the upper stoop. "And don't you go anywhere until I return."

She made it outside through the rain and into her car, thinking about the long drive home. If the house had a few beds, she probably would have stayed. *FBI idiots. They could have rented a furnished house at least.* She backed out of the drive and roared down the street. The good-looking image of Smoke sitting in the recliner was branded in her mind. *Hot chocolate and ice cream.* She shook her head in self-defense. *Don't warm up to him.*

CHAPTER 16

*B*UZZ. *BUZZ. BUZZ.*

Sidney pushed her face out of her pillow and checked the clock on the nightstand. 5:34 a.m. Not even four hours' sleep. With a groan, she sat up. Her eyelids were heavy. She rubbed her neck, stretched out her arms, and yawned.

If that's you, Jack, I'm going to kill you.

Rubbing her eyes, she checked her text messages. There weren't any.

"Great. Phantom buzzing in my sleep now."

She toggled through her features. There was a red update on the tracking app. "What's this?"

She opened it up. Smoke's beacon had moved. It was no longer sitting safely at Benson Park Estates. It was on the move. Miles away. Sidney jumped to her feet.

"Sonuvabitch!"

She stubbed her toe on her bed post.

"Dammit!"

She limped to her closet, grabbed a pair of jeans and a pullover shirt, and slipped them on. She holstered up and tied on her shoes. Inside of two minutes she was squealing out of her parking spot and then back on the road.

She tied her hair back in a ponytail, then rubbed her puffy eyes. It wasn't raining, but the window was frosted up. She rubbed it with her hand and turned up the heater.

"Piece of crap car."

She shivered and checked the beacon. Smoke was moving. West. Toward Annapolis. She laid on the gas.

I'll intercept him in the Interceptor. She laughed. It was a long-standing joke that cops and agents made about the old cars. *Then I'll kill him*.

Hankering for coffee and listening to the moan in her stomach, she plowed down the road. She was angry. Jack. Cyrus. Smoke. They all made her mad. Each was unreliable. Unpredictable. She didn't like it. But she didn't mind the excitement that came with it.

I'll show 'em.

She eased back in her seat and turned on some talk radio. The aggravating conversations were certain to keep her alert. Awake. Promises and failures. A chronic rinse-and-repeat cycle of wasted taxpayer dollars.

Clear your mind, Sid. Focus.

There were a lot of things to take in. Change was one of them. She didn't like change. She liked routine. She liked a plan.

"Some things you just can't plan for," her father often said. "Always assume everything is out of your control, aside from yourself."

She hated it when he said that, right along with the smile that came with it. It made her feel like she was doing something wrong. She did things right. She saw to it others did things right as well.

Cruising down the road, she regained her focus. She'd been off her game.

Too much time behind the desk.

She had yelled and cussed. It showed a lack of self-control.

No more of that. You're a pro, Sid. Be a pro. No surprises. No letdowns.

She unholstered her Glock, ran her fingers over the barrel, and stuffed it back in the holster.

I need to get to the range.

She felt jumpy. Edgy.

I don't like feeling this way.

The frost on the windows cleared, revealing the moon's bright glow. An eerie haze hung in the sky, concealing parts of it. Up ahead, a pack of animals darted across the highway. She squinted.

"What the heck?"

The dogs were big dark silhouettes padding across the concrete and vanishing over the guard rail and into the woods. A chill went through her.

Those were wolves.

She shook her head. *Maybe coyotes. No, coyotes aren't that big.* She slowed the car down and eased onto the berm. *No. Get after Smoke, Sid. No time to fool around.* She laid the gas back on and zoomed up the road. *Those were wolves, though. I know it.* Ted's words came to mind. *Extraordinary caution.*

Cruising at ninety, she closed in on Smoke's beacon, which had come to a stop off somewhere south of the John Hanson Highway. She took the machine up to ninety-five before slowing for the next exit, then followed the beacon down the greenway beyond the condos and plaza to a lonely stretch of road miles from the nearest highway.

What on earth is he doing out here?

That's when another thought crossed her mind. What if it wasn't him at all? What if one of his crew was leading her on a wild goose chase? It had been at least twenty minutes since his beacon stopped moving.

Erase your doubt. Follow your leads.

The beacon led her down a grave stretch of road that ended in a grove of tall trees. A gravel parking lot greeted her, accompanied by a lone warehouse lit up with neon signs. One sign read Chester's in bright orange and green flames. There were a few motorcycles and muscle cars on the scene. Beer cans and broken glass littered the parking lot.

What is he doing here?

Sidney checked the beacon. She was on target. She brought the Interceptor to a halt a hundred feet from the front doors. Fog was lifting into the early sunrise. A man in jeans and a leather vest lay face down in the parking lot. Fresh blood from a broken nose dripped on the ground. There was a gentle rise in his chest. She took out her weapon and crept to the doorway.

What have you gotten into, Smoke?

Inside the bar she could hear loud hillbilly rock playing.

Just when I thought it couldn't get any worse.

She pushed the door open and peeked inside. A gunshot cracked out.

Blam!

CHAPTER 17

SIDNEY CROUCHED DOWN OUTSIDE THE door.

Blam! Blam!

The shots were coming from inside the warehouse, somewhere above her head. Adrenaline pumped through her veins.

Crash!

Glass rained down into the parking lot from above her head. A man fell onto the hood of an old white Camaro. Groaning, he rolled off the hood and onto the ground.

Sidney peeked up and around the corner. A figure stood looking out of the oversized window pane. It was Smoke.

"Freeze!" she said. He vanished. She turned her attention to the other man, who was stumbling away. He hopped onto a motorcycle and started it up. "FBI! Freeze!"

He revved the engine.

"Don't make my day," she said, pointing her weapon

at him. "The first hole goes in your gas tank. The next hole goes in your head."

He raised his hands over his head. His sagging face was skinned up, and his chin was bleeding.

"Sure thing, lady. Sure thing."

"Aiiyee!" a man screamed.

Sidney turned just in time to see another man flying through the window. He crushed the roof of the Camaro.

Vrooom!

The biker revved up his engine and started to speed out of the parking lot.

Blam! Blam!

Sidney put a bullet in his tank and another in his back tire.

"Get on the ground now!" she said.

The man obeyed.

She bound his legs and wrists with flex-cuffs.

"You didn't have to shoot my bike," he said. "Stupid bi—"

She shoved his face in the ground and rubbed it in the gravel.

"What was that?"

"Nothin'."

Smoke landed on the Camaro's hood, a tall figure in a dark shirt and jeans. He dragged the man who had crunched in the roof to the ground.

Sidney trotted over. "What are you doing?"

Smoke had a dangerous look his eye. He punched the man in the face. *Whap!*

"Taking care of unfinished business."

"Stop!" Sidney said, holding her weapon on him. "Stop now!"

Smoke let go, and the man sagged to the ground.

"Who is he?" Sidney watched the man gather himself into a sitting position.

The man was in his forties, shaven head and black bearded. Dusky skinned. Tattoos covered his naked arms. He was thickset. Formidable. Valuable rings dressed his fingers below all of the knuckles except for two of them. His trigger fingers were missing.

"Ray Cline?"

"Sting Ray," Ray interrupted, spitting blood. "You're going to die, Smoke. Die in a horrible way! Oof!"

Smoke kicked him in the gut.

"What was that, Ray? Say, how did that hit that you put on me go down, in prison? Not so well, did it?"

"Back off," Sidney stepped between them, keeping her eyes on Ray. She had become familiar with his file when she studied up on Smoke. He was a killer. A drug lord. A career criminal. For some insane reason, the system had let him out. "I'll handle this."

Ray started laughing.

"You want to handle me, Pretty?" He winked at her. Blood dripped off his chin. "Help yourself then."

She handed Smoke another pair of flex cuffs and covered Ray with her weapon.

"Secure him."

Smoke slipped the flex cuffs around Ray's neck.

"No, no, no!" Ray said.

"Yes, yes, yes," Smoke replied.

"No," Sidney said. "Just the wrists."

"I can make it look like an accident," Smoke said.

"The wrists," Sidney said. "Take care of it while I call this in."

"Wait," Smoke said, cuffing Ray's wrists behind his back. "Before you do that, let me show you something."

"Yeah," Ray said, "let me show you something too, Pretty."

Smoke rabbit-punched Ray's ribs and hauled him up to his feet.

"Not another word, fiend," he said in his ear. "Not another syllable." He shoved Ray back toward the warehouse bar.

"Are you coming or not? You need to see this."

Sidney followed. The intensity in Smoke's voice compelled her. He was angry. It stirred her.

Inside, there was a long bar, a band stage with instruments, high tables scattered about, and a checkered dance floor. Smoke pushed Ray toward a metal stairwell that led up. Two goons were knocked out cold by the threshold.

"Watch your step." Smoke banged Ray's head into the doorframe. "I'd hate to see you get hurt more than you already are." He banged his head into the door frame again. "No, I wouldn't."

At the top of the stairs they entered an office with a large one-way mirror overlooking the dance floor. The furnishings were fine leather and well-crafted oak. A kitchenette. A bar. An apartment of sorts. Bags of cocaine and cash were on a black velvet pool table, along with dozens of small bottles full of pills.

At least a million worth of dope and cash.

Sidney stepped over another prone body, one of three more men whose blood had been spilt on the floor.

"He has a nice little empire here, doesn't he?" Smoke said to her.

"I've seen bigger," she said, "But without probable cause there isn't a case here."

"That's right, Smoke," Ray said with a sneer. "You don't have a case with me, you frigging renegade. You're toast, Smoke."

Smoke shoved Ray onto the sofa and tied his legs to the sofa's foot with the man's belt. One by one, he tore open the cocaine bags and slung them out the window.

"I'm going to kill you, Smoke! Stop doing that!"

"That's evidence," Sidney added.

"Whose side are you on?"

"The law's."

"Yeah, the law's, you stupid bastard," Ray added.

Smoke chucked bundles of cash out the window.

"That's enough," Sidney said, "I'm calling this in."

"Just one more minute," Smoke said, "You haven't seen anything yet." He tilted his head toward another door. "Check there."

She eyed him.

"It's clear. Go ahead."

"Something you want to tell me, Ray?"

The drug lord looked away.

Butterflies started inside her stomach. Smoke's tone. Ray's feverish look. What was on the other side of that office door? She grabbed the brass door knob and shoved it open. A short hallway, maybe twenty feet long, greeted her. A heavy door stood at the end. On the left, or the front side of the warehouse, was an open office with computers. A black man in a biker vest was laid out on the floor. She walked up to the door and glanced back. Smoke stood just outside the doorway.

And behind door number 1 we have...

She pulled open the door and gasped.

CHAPTER 18

CHILDREN WERE INSIDE. SIX IN all. They wore aprons and masks. Wide-eyed, frail and skinny, their hollowed eyes froze on her.

Sidney's heart sank. Blood drained from her face.

The children kept working. Scales. Baggies. Small piles of pills and cocaine. Latex gloves stretched over their little hands. Not a one of them could have been more than ten. Girls and boys. Eyes weak and glassy.

Her knees gave a little. She swallowed. "It's okay. I'm here to help. I'm the police."

A little Latino boy dropped his utensils, ran over, and hugged her. Within seconds, they had all closed in and embraced her. Tears streamed down their faces. Her own eyes watered. Her heart ached. Their lithe bony bodies pressed against hers.

"It's okay. It's okay. Let's find you something to eat." She picked two of them up in her arms. The others hung on her legs and waist. She gently yelled down the hallway, "A little help please."

Smoke picked up a few of the children and took

them into the office. He peeled their tiny fingers off Sidney and set the children down at a table. There was a refrigerator that had some sodas inside. Some Doritos were in the cabinet over the bar. He filled their hands and said, "Eat."

Their fear-filled glances fell on Ray's hard eyes.

Sidney's temperature rose. Her cheeks turned red.

"You're going away for a long, long time, Ray."

"Am I, Pretty? I don't think so. You see, those kids... heh, heh, well, they're all *my* kids."

"I'm sure that isn't so," she said, stepping between Ray and the kids. "I'll see to it this all sticks."

"Good luck with that, Pretty. The only thing that's going to get stuck, though, is you."

Her fingers danced on her gun. She wanted to wound him. Shoot him. Make him pay for all that he'd done.

"You won't shoot me." Ray chuckled. "You have a career. A pension. Hah. You wouldn't want to lose all that, would you."

"True," she said. "But that's not why."

"Really, why is it then?"

"It's because I don't want to set a bad example for the children." She looked at Smoke. "Do you mind removing him from our sight so they can eat in peace?"

"As you wish." Smoke undid the belt, picked Ray up by the scruff of the neck, shoved him toward the outside window, and leaned him over the edge. "Time to fly Smoke Airlines again."

"No! Wait! What are you doing?"

Smoke, much bigger than Ray, hoisted him up over his shoulders.

The whine of police sirens cut through the air.

Sidney rushed to the window.

Three police cruisers pulled into the parking lot. It was the county sheriff.

"Ah ha ha!" Ray laughed. "My cavalry has arrived."

A nagging feeling crept between Sidney's shoulders.

Smoke started to heave Ray out anyway.

Sidney grabbed his shoulder. "No, don't. Put him down." She messed with her phone. "We have to let the law sort this out."

"Amen to that," Ray said. "Amen to—ow!"

Sidney elbowed him in the nose.

The scene was ugly. Sidney had called in her colleagues at the bureau. Ray had called in his the moment Smoke arrived. The two parties fought over jurisdiction. Possession. The children. Smoke was handcuffed in the back of a bureau SUV. The only thing going for them was that nobody had died.

"Stupid, Sid. Really stupid." That was all Jack said when he showed up an hour later. "He needs to go back in the hole."

"I'll handle the paperwork," she said. "It's not that bad. Nobody died. The media hasn't arrived."

"Oh, really. It's not that bad? You have an ex-con going vigilante. You've pissed off the county sheriff's department. I can imagine a dozen lawsuits being filed from all this." He rubbed his forehead. "None of the charges will stick!"

"I can handle it."

"You're what, going to make something up? Lie?"

"No," she sighed, "embellish."

Jack's face turned red. "Embellish!"

"Don't you raise your voice to me, Jack. You saw the drugs. The lab. The children. Don't you act like this can't stick." She poked him in the chest. "We've handled worse. I seem to remember doing a few favors for you."

"Get... get over here." He pulled her away from prying eyes and ears. "Listen to me. You are out of your lane. This is not part of the Black Slate. No, you blew it. Your little soldier over there is going back to the jail cell where he belongs. Experiment over. And you will be spending a lot more time behind the desk."

"Wait a minute. It's only been one day. I'm supposed to have two weeks."

"Tough. Now get in your car, go home, and report back to me in the office tomorrow so you can get started on all the paperwork you wanted."

"No," she argued. "We have a lead on AV."

Jack looked up into the sky and shook his head. "I could almost let this slide." He locked eyes with her. "Except there's another detail you missed. Congressman Wilhelm gave me a call late yesterday, and let's just say it wasn't so pleasant."

Crap!

Congressman Wilhelm was her brain-dead sister's boyfriend Dave's uncle.

"I gave you the benefit of the doubt, Sid. I sympathize with you regarding your sister. But now this?"

"Sir—"

"No sirs, Sid! Go home. It's over." His phone buzzed inside his suit pocket. "Excuse me." Jack walked away.

Sid headed for her car.

I can't believe this!

Smoke sat in the back of a black FBI SUV. She shot eye daggers at him through the tinted windows. She could have sworn he waved.

Good riddance.

Things were beginning to clear up. Ray and his men were gone. The children had been taken by protective services, leaving only a few men from the sheriff's department. One of them passed her by and in a low voice said, "Now you're in the crosshairs. Beware, Agent. Beware."

"What?"

He tipped his cap and kept on moving. Seconds later, the deputy sheriffs and their cruisers were gone, leaving only her, Jack, and Agent Tommy Tohms—and Smoke, but he was locked up. She popped open her car door and started inside.

Well, at least the kids are safe.

"But sir?" she heard Jack exclaim. His face reddened. "But—" He looked at his phone. "Dammit!" He started to throw it on the ground, but stopped short. He marched over to his SUV and opened Smoke's door.

"Get out!"

Smoke eased his big frame out of the car.

"Uncuff him, Tommy."

Smoke handed Tommy the cuffs.

Jack snatched them out of Tommy's hands and slung them away. He pointed his finger in Smoke's face. "Don't get my agent killed, you stupid sonuvabitch. Let's go, Tommy."

"But my cuffs!"

"Let's go!" Jack glared at Sid. "You got your wish, Sid. He's all yours."

Ten seconds later, Smoke and Sidney stood in the parking lot all alone.

She got into her car, feeling a little bit elated.

Smoke joined her.

"I have one question," she said.

"Shoot."

"How in the hell did you get here?"

CHAPTER 19

"**H**UNGRY?" SMOKE ASKED.

Sidney rolled her eyes. She was torn between mad and happy.

Smoke patted his belly. "I always get hungry after an adventure like that."

"I don't care." She accelerated up the highway.

"It's early. I know a diner around here that makes great pancakes."

"No."

"Excellent coffee too."

Yes.

"No."

"Come on, Agent Shaw. You can't be that sore at me. We did a good thing back there."

"'Sore at you?' Really? Is this the nineteen fifties? Who says that anymore?"

"I picked it up from some old timer in prison. He said that a lot. 'Don't be sore at me, boss.' It kind of stuck." He popped open the glove box. "Got any snacks in here?"

She leaned over and slammed the glove box shut.

"No."

Smoke shrugged. He adjusted his seat backward, locked his fingers behind his head, and closed his eyes. Seconds later he was snoring.

You have got to be kidding me!

She glanced over at him. His athletic frame filled out his black T-shirt and jeans. His knuckles were scuffed and swollen, and there were white scars on his bare arms.

He wouldn't be so bad if I didn't hate him.

She backhanded him in the chest.

He lurched up. "What—what?"

"You're on duty. No sleeping."

"So now we're a team, are we?"

"Where's the diner you were talking about?"

Smoke's dark eyes scanned the signs on the highway. He rubbed his jaw. "Two more exits. You'll love it."

"We'll see."

The diner wasn't much, but the silverware was clean. It was an old dining car in the front with much more built on in the back. Blue stools hugged the chrome-trimmed counter. The floor was hardwood, and the booth they sat in was a soft blue vinyl. A gas fireplace burned at one end. It was warm. Cozy.

"Nice, isn't it?" Smoke stuffed in a mouthful of pancakes that looked like they were stacked to his chin. "Ever seen a fireplace in a dining car?"

Sidney picked through her eggs and bacon. "No." She took a sip of coffee. *Mmmm… good coffee.*

"How's the coffee?"

"It's all right."

"Would you like to try my pancakes?"

Yes.

"No." She scraped up the rest of her eggs and washed them down. "Are you about finished?"

Smoke looked at his stack. "No. Are we in a hurry?"

"Yes."

"For what? AV isn't supposed to show until five. We have plenty of time." He flagged down the waitress. "Could I get another Coke, please?"

"Sure thing."

"I'm still catching up from prison time," Smoke said to her. "I hope you don't mind, but I'm hungry."

"Fine, take your time." She checked the messages on her phone. "You clearly know what you're doing. And your friend, Ray, when he's released—say, tomorrow— will be thankful for your intervention."

"It wasn't supposed to go down that way."

"Really?" She leaned forward and looked him in the eye. "And how was it supposed to go down?"

"You weren't supposed to show up." He cut up his sausage and pointed at her with it on his fork. "I had it all under control. I told you, just leave me be."

No.

"All right, so I don't show up, what happens?"

"I have my ways. I nullify Ray and his gang and secure the kids." The waitress returned and put his Coke on the table. "Thanks. The kids are the main thing. Once they're safe, I burn the place down."

"Arson? That was your brilliant plan. Committing a felony."

"I'm just kidding."

She shook her head. "No, no you aren't."

"Come on." He tried to catch her eye. "You know you feel good that we put some bad guys down and saved some kids. Everyone is better off now."

She balled up her fist and said through her teeth, "That wasn't our mission."

"He put a hit out on me. He's slime. Do you have any idea how many people have disappeared under his watch?"

"That's not the point."

"How many women and children?"

"You don't know that."

"Yes, yes I do. I studied him for months. I have files inches thick I can show you." He reached over and grabbed her arm. "Justice was served today, and it didn't take a pile of paperwork to dispense it."

His grip was warm and strong. She pulled away.

"Let's go."

"But I'm not finished."

She tossed two twenties on the table. "You are now."

CHAPTER 20

THE DRAKE. THAT WAS WHERE Rod had said AV would be. It wasn't at all what Sidney expected.

"That's different," Smoke said.

A series of barges formed a small city along the Potomac on the Virginia side of the river, south of the Torpedo Art Museum. A lighthouse could be seen in the distance. Standing on the wharf that jutted over the river and led to the barrages was a lone sign that pointed to the Drake.

"Let's go," Sidney said.

The Drake was a hotel-like building that sat on top of the backs of four barges. Pleasant music drifted down the pier that ran alongside it. The salivating scent of food drifted into her nostrils. She led with Smoke in tow, drifting in with the crowd that traversed the docks. Along with the hotel/restaurant getaway there were small stores and local artists. Beatniks, preppies, hippies, all sorts walked, talked and made polite conversation.

"Great," she said. A long line of people had formed outside the restaurant at the Drake.

"Shall I put our name on the list?" Smoke said.

"No, let's go around. Come on."

The Drake plaza sat on a huge boardwalk and deck. People gathered around the railing watching the boats and ferries. A few hard faces fished. A staircase led down to a boat dock and slips on the back of the floating city. Men in dark suits stood on the docks, helping men and women from their boats. Sidney could see the bulges of body holsters concealed under their jackets.

"Pretty seedy," Smoke said.

Sidney took a closer look at the men fishing. They were holstered up too. And so were some of the common folk milling about. She counted at least ten well-armed men and women. Guns for hire. Bodyguards. Goons.

"I'll be. We're on private property," she said under her breath.

"Yep," Smoke said. "It seems like AV has thought of everything. A criminal's safe house. An excellent escape route with immediate access to three states. I like it."

"It seems you convicts all think alike." She smiled up at him and hooked her arm in his. "Oh, don't frown. Buy a girl a drink, why don't you." She tugged him along. "Come on. We can't make our intentions obvious."

"I don't have any cash."

"And that's why there won't be a second date." They made their way up to the hostess stand.

"Name and how many?" the hostess said.

Sidney looked up at Smoke.

"Er, two, and the last name is Ferrigno."

The young waitress wrote it down and handed him a pager. "Okay, it will be at least an hour, Mister Ferrigno.

113

You can get some drinks on the plaza while you wait."
She smiled. "Next."

They grabbed two long-necks from a beer stand and
took a seat on a bench overlooking the river.

"A toast," Smoke said.

"No."

"I'm just trying to act natural," he said. "Forgive me;
I haven't been on a date in a while."

"This isn't a date." She took a sip of beer. "And don't
get wasted on that beer. I might need you."

"Really?"

"It's a figure of speech."

"If you say so." He tilted the bottle to his lips and
guzzled it down. "Ah!"

"What did I just say?"

"What? I've been in prison. Can you blame me?"

"No more." She eased back on the bench and crossed
her legs. The chill from the river was worse than she
expected. It was a starry night. "This place is full of all
kinds of everything."

"It sure is." Smoke cleared his throat. "I wonder who
Drake is?"

"I only care who AV is. You should too."

A group of men in tuxedos with women in fine jewels
crested the steps that led down to the dock. Eyes forward
and faces drawn tight, they marched straight for the
restaurant.

"I'll be."

"What?"

One of the men was Congressman Wilhelm, with his
troupe of lackeys. His beady eyes turned her way. There
was no avoiding his gaze.

She nudged Smoke.

"Kiss me."

"Wh—"

She pulled his face down to hers and locked her lips with his. He pulled her body into his. A charge went through her.

Good kisser. Three. Two. One. Through the corner of her eye, she saw Congressman Wilhelm move on. She held the kiss a moment longer and broke it off. "That'll do."

"Do you mind telling what that was all about?"

"Yes, I do mind." *What is Wilhelm doing here?*

"Ex-boyfriend?"

"No."

"Animal attraction?"

"Don't get any ideas. I might explain later."

Locking his fingers behind his head, he gazed upward into the stars. "Oh, at least you've given me plenty to think about."

Me too.

Smoke pulled the flashing pager out of his pocket. "That was quick."

"Sure was." Sidney felt eyes on her and noticed a few cameras on the lamp posts. A pair of eyes along the railing drifted away from her. A woman at the beer stand spoke into her wrist and looked away. "I have a feeling Rod Brown gave us up."

"Maybe." Smoke cracked his knuckles. "Say, are you going to finish that beer?"

She took a long drink and handed it over. "Knock yourself out."

Smoke chugged it down. "Ah!"

Please don't burp.

"Buuuurp! Whoa!" Smoke tapped his chest. "Sorry."

Sidney got up and started toward the restaurant. A mix of six men and women wearing dark pea coats hemmed them in with hands on their holsters.

CHAPTER 21

A DUSKY-SKINNED WOMAN WITH DARK CORNROWS stepped forward, rolling a toothpick from one side of her mouth to the other. She had a hard edge in her voice.

"My name is Gina. I speak on behalf of the Drake. You need to leave."

"I beg your pardon, Gina?"

"Listen, Miss." The woman rolled the toothpick to the other side of her mouth. "This is private property. The Drake Management doesn't want you here."

"I don't follow." Sidney glanced at the tattoos crawling up the rough-cut woman's neck.

"I don't need to explain myself. I know you saw the private property lines. You're trespassing."

No, I'm getting close to something. AV must be here.

The woman stuck her fist inside her palm and cracked her knuckles. "Now, I'm asking nicely. Don't make me mess up that pretty little face of yours." She cracked her neck from side to side. "I'd love to do it."

"I'm certain that's not going to happen."

Gina took a step closer and leaned forward. "Listen, tramp, I've busted up men and women in the octagon. These hands are lethal weapons. And here, heh, well, I'm free to use them. I've left the bloodstains of my victims on the deck before. Just ask them." She tipped her chin. "What do you think about that, Pretty?"

"I don't think a woman acting like a man makes for much of a woman."

Gina's eyes enlarged. "What!" She shoved Sidney in the chest.

Sidney absorbed the push, lowered her hip, and launched a roundhouse kick. She caught Gina flush on the chin. Gina smacked the deck face first, spilling her blood.

The men closed in with fingers itching on their weapons.

Sidney whipped out her badge. "FBI, back off!"

The wary-eyed men eased back.

"Her assault on a federal officer just gave me probable cause to search this place. Come on." She led Smoke through the gathering crowd. "He's in there. I can feel it." She rushed past the hostess stand.

Smoke tossed the hostess the pager. "The Ferrignos will be seating themselves tonight."

Sidney carefully picked her way through the tables while scanning the crowd. The Drake had two levels: the main floor of booths and tables decorated in a high-décor riverboat look, and the upstairs level, which was roped off for private parties.

"Up there." Sidney eyed a man who was quickly moving along the balcony. He spoke to another group of men who were seated. It was Congressman Wilhelm and his party. Sidney stepped under the balcony, evading their concerned glances.

"The only way out of here is back the way we came. I didn't notice a fire escape. Did you?"

Smoke was at her side. He peeked up at the next level. "Apparently the Drake doesn't like OSHA, either. I saw him."

Sidney pulled him back. "Saw who?"

"AV. He's up there at your ex-boyfriend's table."

Some of the goons in pea coats eased their way into the restaurant without creating a commotion.

"Are you sure you saw him?"

"Yep."

"Let's go up then." Heading for the stairs, she was cut off by a bald thickset bodyguard in a dark grey suit. She flashed her badge. "I need to get a message to Congressman Wilhelm. It's urgent federal business."

He took a hard look and glanced up at the balcony. Someone gave him a nod. He removed the velvet rope and stepped aside. "Go on up. But just you, lady."

Smoke's fist crashed into the man's rugged jaw.

Whop!

The henchman sagged onto the stairs.

Up they went, side by side. At the top, two other henchmen awaited them. Sidney's fingertips danced on her weapon. "Move."

The pair of men parted, and at the top a table awaited with eight guests. One of them was Congressman Wilhelm. The other face she recognized was Adam Vaughn's.

"Agent Shaw," Congressman Wilhelm said, lighting up a cigar, "may I ask what you are doing here?"

"I could ask you the same," she said.

"I don't answer to anyone less than a senator."

"I'm sure your voters would love to hear that."

The congressman chuckled. "They only hear what I want them to hear." He squeezed his date's knee with the hand bearing his wedding ring. "And they only believe what I want them to believe."

A few more henchmen crowded near the table. Congressman Wilhelm had a secret service agent on one side and his baby-doll date on the other. One seat over from AV, Rod Brown sat in a blue suit, eyeing a spot on the table.

"As always," Sidney said, "you seem to be on top of things, so I assume you know you're dining with a wanted man?"

"Beg pardon?" Wilhelm's eyes slid toward AV, but shifted back to her. "What are you talking about? You're not here to pester me?"

"No," she said, taking out her flex cuffs, "I'm here for Adam Vaughn."

"Adam? What on earth would you want with Adam?"

Adam Vaughn's fine features darkened. His eyes scoured his men.

"That isn't any of your business, Congressman. But I'm sure your spineless sources will fill you in soon enough. Mister Vaughn, I need you to come with me."

"Stay put, Adam," Wilhelm said, tossing his napkin on the table and getting up from his seat. "You listen to me, Shaw. You need to get out of here. Get out of here now. You're in deeper than you know." He plucked out his phone and started to dial. "Relax, Adam. I'll handle this."

Adam Vaughn was an attractive man, small in stature, with a head of coarse black hair and heavy eyebrows. He wore a white shirt with an open collar underneath a blue pin-striped suit. His eyes narrowed and his jaws were clenching. The atmosphere was ripe with tension. Sidney felt Smoke slide in behind her. She glanced back. His eyes were laser locked on AV.

"Let's go, Mister Vaughn," she said, using more authority this time.

AV had turned his attention to Rod. The big man's head was beaded with sweat.

"Rod," AV said in a European accent that was more deadly than charming, "look at me."

Rod lifted his chin, started to turn, and began shaking uncontrollably.

"I'm sorry, AV. I'm sorry!"

"Nobody's sorry, Adam," Wilhelm said, covering his phone. "I'll take care of this in a moment." He rolled his eyes at Sidney. "You really don't know what's good for you."

"Betrayer!" Adam jumped up from his seat and lunged at Rod.

Sidney drew her weapon. "Back off, Mister Vaughn!"

AV lifted his palms and backed off. "You're dead to me, Rod." He spat on the table. "Dead!" He came out from behind the table and faced Sidney. "You'll soon be dead to me too."

"Turn around — *oof!*"

AV kicked her in the gut, dropping her to her knees. He ducked under Smoke's lunging arms and leaped over the rail and crashed onto a table below. A cry of alarm went up all over the restaurant.

Smoke catapulted off the rail and charged after AV, who was dashing toward the exit.

Sidney scrambled to her feet and headed for the stairs, tripping over Wilhelm's feet.

"Watch your step, Agent Shaw," he said with a sinister grin. "Watch your step."

CHAPTER 22

SIDNEY HIT THE LANDING AT the bottom of the steps just as Smoke vanished through the front doors. Panicked people spilled into her way.

"Move it!"

A path slowly parted between feeble bodies and bewildered faces. She powered through them, shoving a man and two women down. "Does anyone know what move means?"

While she was rushing by the hostess stand, two peacock goons blocked her path. She blasted two warning shots into the floor.

Blam! Blam!

One goon dove left and the other dove right. Everybody screamed. Through the door Sidney went. Sprinting on long, fast legs, she surged out onto the deck and saw Smoke racing through the crowd thirty yards away. AV vanished down the steps leading to the docks. Smoke disappeared right after him.

Get down there, Sid!

At the top of the stairs, two more gunshots cracked

off. The bodyguard on the dock was blasting away at the slithery Smoke.

Sidney took aim.

Blam!

Her bullet ripped through the back of the man's shoulder, spinning him to the ground. Down the stairs she went, sidestepping the big man and kicking his pistol into the water. After Smoke and AV she went, weapon ready. A pitch-black 30-foot cabin cruiser at the end of the dock started pulling out of its slip.

No you don't! She sprinted toward the end of the dock. *Faster, Sid! Faster!* Adrenaline surging through her limbs, she put everything into her jump. She sailed through the air. *I'm going to make it!*

Her foot clipped the edge of the boat, making for an ugly landing. She tumbled and bumped her head on the table. Bright starry spots drew in her eyes. She rubbed her head and forced herself up to her feet. A man in a captain's hat was up the stairs behind the wheel. She took aim and said, "FBI! Shut it down!"

The man remained unmoving. Sidney went up the steps and put the gun to his neck.

"I said, shut it down."

The man turned to face her. His face was pasty, hair ratty and stringy, eyes hollow and lifeless.

She gasped. Something evil, unnatural lurked behind his sunken eyes.

In a burst, the creepy man shoved her aside and lumbered stiffly down the stairs.

"Freeze!"

He kept going.

She fired a round at his leg.

Blam!

Unfazed, he stepped up on the edge of the boat and fell into the black water.

Sidney rushed down the steps and looked over the rail. The man was gone. Only the captain's hat remained afloat.

I know I hit him... it.

"Sid!" a voice cried out. "Sid!"

She twisted around. Smoke's voice was coming from inside the lower cabin. She burst through the doors. Smoke's big frame had AV pinned down on the floor. The smaller man twisted away and sprinted toward Sidney. Smoke tackled his legs and launched a quick punch in AV's ribs. The man sagged.

"Cuffs!" Smoke said, chest heaving.

"What?"

"Flex cuffs!" he added, sucking for air. He wrenched AV's arms behind his back.

AV jerked them away.

"You are one strong little man!" Smoke punched both sides of his ribs again. *Whap! Whap!* "I'll have no more of that, you swarthy Spaniard."

"I'm not Spanish, you fool!" AV spat on the floor. "I'm something else."

You're something else, all right.

Sidney kneeled down and put her gun barrel to AV's temple. "If you don't remain still, something else of yours is going to be splattered all over the floor."

AV's struggles eased. He gazed up at her. His eyes were black pools. Insidious. Primal. Evil. Hair rose on her neck. Without averting her eyes, she handed Smoke the cuffs. He crisscrossed AV's wrists and bound them.

"Do you have another pair?"

"I always have another pair," she said, handing them over.

Smoke tied down AV's legs, leaned back against the bed, and caught his breath.

Winded herself, Sidney sat back on the steps and wiped her sleeve across her forehead. She then asked AV, "Is there anyone else on this boat we should know about?"

"Do you see anyone else?" he said with a sneer. "It's just me and a couple of soon-to-be dead people."

Smoke kicked him. "Where's the captain?"

"He jumped overboard."

"Really?" Smoke said, cocking his ear, "then who's driving the boat?"

The blaring sound of a boat horn ripped through the chill night air.

Sidney's eyes widened. She jumped to her feet, darted up the stairs, and raced up to the captain's chair. A river barge was almost on top of them. She spun the wheel right and pumped down the throttle. The fore of the boat rose high, and the propellers sank the aft of the boat into the water. Sidney hung onto the wheel. The massive bulk of the barge cruised by with little more than a foot to spare.

That was close.

She throttled down the cruiser and watched the barge pass by.

Too close.

She scanned the black water. The barge's wake beat against the hull. There was no sign of the captain— and she was certain the captain wasn't any man at all. Cruising down the shoreline, she caught movement along the bank. A drenched figure lumbered out of the water, up the shore, and disappeared into the woods. A chill went through her.

That's wasn't a man. I swear it!

CHAPTER 23

"EXCELLENT JOB, SID," SAID JACK Dydeck. "Just excellent." He paced the floor with his fingers locked behind his back. They were back at the house: Jack, Tommy Tohms, Sidney, Smoke, and a couple of other agents. AV sat cross-legged, head down, by the fireplace. "You erased a name on the Black Slate in one day?" He put his hand on her shoulder and squeezed it. "I'm proud of you, Sid."

"There's really no need. It's my job, and I can't take all the credit." She nodded at Smoke. "He helped."

Smoke sat quietly on the sofa, eyes intent on AV. He hadn't said much of anything since they journeyed back from the Potomac and Jack and his men picked them up.

"I'm sure he did," Jack said. "We'll be sure to send him some new books to read back in prison."

"Wait," Sidney said, "I thought we had two weeks?"

"Sure, to get Mister Vaughn here. That's all over now."

"Hold on." Sidney was not hiding the irritation in her

voice. "There are reports. Interrogations. Investigations of his operations. The list goes on. I want to be thorough."

"We'll handle that, Sid. You go get some rest and we'll talk tomorrow."

"No, I'll handle it."

Jack offered a smile. "Tomorrow. Back in the office. Around noon. We'll await Mister Vaughn's caretakers." His tone became stern. "You look exhausted, Sid. We can stitch up this mess tomorrow. Go."

"What about him?" She looked at Smoke.

Jack sighed.

"Tell you what: seeing how the two of you caught headquarters with their pants down, well," he scratched his head, "they aren't sure what the next step is. I'm waiting on their call to advise me on what to do with Mister Smoke, so the two of you head up the road and grab a bite to eat. I'll call you back after Mister Vaughn is picked up. We'll take it from there. Fair enough?"

"I'd rather stay," Smoke said. His eyes were still glued on AV.

"I don't care." Jack glowered at him. "You can go eat or sit here handcuffed."

"Come on," Sidney said to Smoke. "Let's go."

Slowly, Smoke rose from the sofa and headed out the door. Sidney was one half-step behind.

"Give us a couple of hours, Sid," Jack said. "I should have it all wrapped up by then."

"All right," she said, glancing down at AV.

His eyes fastened on hers. "Soon, Pretty. Soon."

Goosebumps rose on her arms. She tore her gaze away and went back outside. She was short of breath.

"You okay?" Smoke said.

She swallowed and took a breath. "Yeah. Let's go."

"You've been awfully quiet," Sidney said to Smoke. They were sitting in a truck stop restaurant almost ten miles up the road from the house. Smoke's burger and fries were getting cold. "Did you lose your appetite?"

"Tell me about that captain again."

"I don't know." She covered her yawn. "It was dark. I've been tired." She took a sip of coffee. "His face was clammy. Veiny. Like a, well, I don't know."

"Like a zombie?"

"I wouldn't take it that far." She wrinkled her forehead. "Zombies don't drive boats. It might have been sick from something."

"You said *it* again."

"Him. It. It was ugly. Ugh. He was ugly. Just let it go."

"But you said you shot him. Hit his leg. But didn't slow him."

"Adrenaline."

"You said he walked up the shore and disappeared."

"It might have been someone else. It was too far to see."

"I don't think anyone else would have been swimming in the Potomac." Smoke pushed his plate aside, scooted back into the booth, and stretched his legs out.

"Make yourself comfortable, why don't you."

Smoke closed his eyes and rubbed his temples.

He's getting weird on me.

"Are you all right?"

"I have a confession." His eyes were still closed.

Oh great. Please don't give me some sappy story about the last time you ate Pop-tarts with your sister.

"Great. There's a Catholic steeple down the street."

"I'm worried." He opened his eyes and looked worried.

"So?"

"I don't get worried."

"Well, I guess you're just one of us now."

"AV. He's not normal."

"No, most criminals aren't. What's the matter? Are you afraid he won't be a good cell mate?"

Smoke raised his eyebrows at her.

"Sorry. That was uncalled for." She leaned forward. "It's been a really long day."

"Agent Shaw, did you get a good look when AV jumped off the balcony?"

"I was there."

"Well, so was I. There aren't many people aside from Olympic athletes who can jump that far in a single bound." He sat up. "He made a mistake and ran for the boat, thinking the bodyguards would stop us. If he had run into the city, we never would have caught him."

"So he's fast."

"And strong." Smoke narrowed his eyes at her. "I have a hundred pounds on him. It took all I had to wrestle him down."

"He's in shape. Adrenaline. Maybe he's on something. That wouldn't be a first. My father told me he saw a man on PCP burst out of his handcuffs once."

"No," Smoke said in a hushed voice, "I'm telling you, he's not normal. Just like that captain isn't normal."

"Don't overthink it." She finished off her coffee and checked her phone. No messages from Jack yet, and it had been two hours. She yawned. "I wonder why this is taking so long."

Smoke started to ease himself out of the booth. "I say we head back." His eyes were restless. "I have a bad feeling."

Can't disagree there. But I'm not going to let him spook me either.

"Sure, why not." Sid fetched some bills out of her bag. "Do you want a doggie bag?"

"What?"

She dropped the money on the table. "Lighten up a little, will you?"

Driving down the road, Sid couldn't shake the butterflies from her stomach. Smoke was uncomfortable. It made her uncomfortable.

What is his deal?

She'd texted Dydeck before they left and hadn't heard back. Jack was always quick to reply. Ahead, the half-moon shone brightly behind the rising mist of the late evening. She barreled down the exit ramp, merged onto the highway, cruised a few more miles down the road, and turned into Benson Estates.

A pack of dogs darted across the road. Sidney slammed on the brakes. Her heart was jumping.

"Whoa." Smoke leaned forward in his seat. "Were those coyotes?"

"Coyotes aren't that big," Sidney said, peering into the night. The pack had vanished behind the houses. "Those were wolves."

"Like timber wolves? I don't know about that. But they were big. Shepherds, maybe."

"Wolves, trust me. I'm pretty familiar with the breeds of dogs." She let off the brake pedal and eased on up the road. It was the second time she'd seen them in a day.

"Care to fill me in?"

"No."

"So, you used to be a veterinarian?"

She didn't reply.

"Really? Is it that hard to share the smallest detail of any of your history?"

"No. I'm just staying focused right now." Driving slowly, she surveyed between the houses they passed. "Just keeping it professional."

"I agree, but I think you should work on tuning up your social skills."

After a long pause, Sidney said, "I was a K-9 cop in the Air Force."

"Oh." Smoke nodded. He sniffed the air. "Funny, you don't smell like a canine cop. They usually have a scent about them."

"I'm not one now, obviously."

"Just a little humor, Agent Shaw. Take it easy."

She almost cracked a smile as she pulled the car alongside the curb of the house. The two black SUVs were still in the driveway.

Unbuckling his belt and getting out of the car, Smoke said, "It doesn't look like anyone else has shown up." He headed for the front door. Sidney followed in step behind him. The lights were on inside. The front door was wide open. No sounds came from within. "That's weird."

"Sure is," she said, drawing her weapon.

Smoke stopped at the threshold. His arms fanned out, shielding her.

"Wait."

Sidney's body tingled with tiny fires. She slipped underneath Smoke's arm and stepped inside. Blood dripped from the fireplace mantle. The stench of death was thick. She gasped.

CHAPTER 24

S IDNEY STUMBLED BACK INTO SMOKE, mumbling, "No... no."

Blood pooled on the floor. Splattered on the walls. Two agents lay in mangled heaps of flesh. A man was disemboweled, his frozen gaze fixed on the hearth. It was Tommy Tohms. A woman lay with her elbow and neck snapped. The third agent sat on the sofa, coated in blood. His head was missing. Twisted clean off.

Sidney swallowed hard and choked out a cry when she saw the head lying on the fireplace grate. It was Dydeck.

She started shaking. This was inhuman. Uncanny. She dropped her weapon. Her knees sagged.

Smoke caught her. "Let's get you to the car."

"No." She gasped, wiped the tears from her eyes, reached down to pick up her weapon, and took a deep breath. "I can handle this."

"This is madness. Not a lot of people can handle madness."

Sidney took another deep breath and straightened

herself. "Not a lot of people can handle me mad either. Let's get to the bottom of this."

AV was gone. Sidney noticed the busted flex cuffs on the floor.

Smoke was squatted down, eyeballing them. "These weren't cut, they were torn," he said, covering his nose. "Whew... Death stinks."

Sidney held her stomach.

Don't puke. Don't puke.

Blood coated the walls in the living room. It dripped from the ceiling. It looked like a Cuisinart had ripped through the agents in the room.

"What could have done this?" she asked herself.

"These are claw marks. A wild pack of canines perhaps."

"Dogs wouldn't do this."

She studied Dydeck's headless corpse. She'd lost a few friends in the field, but none that she knew well. Her heart ached. Dydeck had a wife and three children.

Lord, no. Lord, no. This can't happen. Not like this. Not to Dydeck.

He was hard-nosed. Not always right. But she liked him. She liked him a lot.

Dydeck still had his weapon in hand. It had been discharged. She turned. The same with Tommy Tohms.

"Do you see any bullet holes?" She pulled some latex gloves from her inside pocket and checked the cartridge on Dydeck's weapon. It was empty.

He couldn't have missed. Not at this close a range.

"Two in the wall over here," Smoke said, fingering the holes, "and one nick in the mantle."

"There should be more," Sidney said, brushing the hair from her eyes. "This magazine is empty."

"I don't see anything else," Smoke said. "They must have filled something with lead."

Sidney noticed a pair of holes on the blood-stained floor.

"Here's another. Geez." She took out her phone and dialed headquarters. It wasn't her first instinct, but it was protocol. She wanted to call Ted, her old boss. A woman's voice answered.

"This is Agent Sidney Shaw—"

She heard the squeal of brakes and pushed the blinds up.

"Hold on."

An unmarked black van had pulled into the driveway. Four men in FBI jackets came out and slammed the doors shut.

One of them was Cyrus. "Agents down. More agents arriving on scene at 241 Benson Estates. Send forensic team and homicide." Cyrus spilled in the doorway and stopped in his tracks. His eyes widened and his face turned ashen. "What the hell?" He jerked out his weapon and pointed it at Smoke. "Freeze!"

Smoke raised his arms over his head.

"Cyrus." Sidney cut in between the two men. "They were dead when we got here. Lower your weapon."

Three other agents poured into the room with their weapons drawn.

"Did you clear the house?" Cyrus said.

"Not yet, I just got—"

"Secure the house," Cyrus ordered his men. "Now!

You," he said to Smoke. "Don't move." He grabbed one of the agents by the sleeve and said, "Cuff him."

"That's not necessary," Sidney objected. "He's done nothing wrong."

Smoke's arms were jerked behind his back and he was shackled. "Don't forget to double-lock them," he said.

"Stay with him," Cyrus said to the other agents. He looked at Sidney. "You, come with me." His eyes drifted toward the fireplace. He blinked and leaned in. "Is that… Dydeck?"

"Yes," she said. "Cyrus, I just arrived a few minutes before you. How come the transport was late? It should have been here over an hour ago to take Adam Vaughn away."

"Sir," one of the agents said, coming from downstairs. "We have another agent down, but she's breathing. The rest of the home is secure."

"Call an ambulance," Cyrus said, rushing down the hall and down the steps.

Sidney was right on his heels. At the bottom of the stairs a woman in an FBI vest lay still. Sidney swallowed. The agent—a short-haired black lady—was crumpled up in a heap.

"Back broken," said one of the agents, a short wiry man with a mustache. He shook his head. "Probably from the fall. A bad spill." He patted her leg. "Hang on, honey. Hang on."

"Don't touch her," Cyrus said, kneeling by the woman's side. "Wait for the ambulance to arrive."

"She didn't fall," Sidney said, gazing at the stairwell. There was a large indentation in the drywall. "She was thrown."

Cyrus stood up, glanced up the stairwell, and said, "That's not possible." He eyed the spot. "Maybe it was already there."

"I don't think so," Sidney said.

"Well, I don't care what you think, Agent Shaw." Cyrus's forehead started to bead with sweat. "Forensics will decide that. You need to decide how to explain all this."

"Me?"

He got in her face. "Yes, you!"

"Hey, Cyrus," the short agent said, "look at this."

Cyrus took out a pair of glasses and put them on. "What is it?"

"She has something in her hand," the agent said. "It looks like hair."

Sidney leaned in. The hair was long, dark brown, and very coarse. Cyrus scooted over and blocked her view. She said, "Do you mind?"

"As a matter of fact, I do." He rose up, stood in front of her, and pointed up the stairs. "Go."

"I beg your pardon?"

"I'm the senior agent on the scene," he said. "And you are going."

"Going where?"

"Going home."

CHAPTER 25

WHAP! WHAP! WHAP!
Sidney laid into the heavy bag that hung in the gym.

Whap! Whap!

Sweat dripped from her brow.

Whap!

Chest heaving inside her Under-Armor hoodie, she walked over to a nearby bench and twisted the cap off her bottled water. It was Saturday, two days after the massacre at Benson Estates. She'd spent all day Friday doing paperwork, and she hadn't heard a word about the case since. Cyrus didn't return her texts. He'd iced her. She finished off her water, crushed the bottle, and tossed it in a can. *Damn him.*

The gym had a little bit of everything going on and was fairly busy for a Saturday. Men and women pushed weighted sleds. Cross trainers pushed their clients to the limits. Sweating bodies churned on treadmills and elliptical machines lined up row-by-row in front of the wall-mounted television. The entire gym smelled like sweat, and the music playing gave it energy.

She ripped a sidekick into the bag. Launched another and another.

A man walking by stopped and watched. He was a little shorter than her, red-faced, and all muscle in a little T-shirt. Tattoos of daggers and snakes decorated his shoulders. He nodded and smiled. "You really know how to work that bag. Impressive."

Great. "Thanks." She paused. "Are you waiting?"

"No," he said, shaking his chin. "I'm enjoying watching." He looked her up and down. "You really are something. How long have you been working out?"

"Listen—"

"Tommy. Tommy's my name." He extended his hand. "Weightlifting is my game."

She laughed. "Tommy, you really need to go."

"I can't leave without your name."

She walked over the padded floor to her gym bag, grabbed her badge, and held it in front of Tommy's widened eyes. "Here are my initials. Now beat it."

He eased back but kept smiling. "Well, FBI, you are one fine agent. You can cuff me any time."

"Can I shoot you too?"

He swallowed. "Er... No." He blinked a couple of times, turned, and walked away.

Loser.

Sidney worked the bag again. Combos of kicks and punches. She loved kick boxing. It had been a passion of hers since she was nine. Her arms became heavy. Her black stretch pants were soaked in sweat. She unleashed some more roundhouse kicks.

Whap! Whap! WHAP!

She took the sparring gloves off, tossed them into her gym bag, and headed toward the treadmills. The ghastly images from the crime scene still burned in her mind. Dydeck was dead. Good agents were dead. One paralyzed. And somewhere, a killer was out there running free. Could it have been Adam Vaughn? It wasn't possible. But that wasn't what bothered her most.

Smoke was gone.

She climbed up on a step mill, punched in the time and intensity, and started walking.

Things had gotten ugly between her and Cyrus when he'd told her to leave. She had objected. The mousy man with frosty eyes had responded by having Smoke carted off behind her back, with no goodbyes between them.

"Your boyfriend is headed back to prison. You'll have to get your kiss goodbye some other place, some other time."

It gnawed at her gut. After a forty-five-minute workout, it still stuck in her craw.

Maybe I should go for a run. Or go shooting.

She gathered her things and exited the gym into the biting wind, headed for her car. The Interceptor wasn't alone. A man wearing a brown leather Donegal and a tweed trench stood there.

"Ted?" She looked around the parking lot. "What are you doing here?"

"I just came to see how you were doing."

"Really." She unlocked the car and tossed her gym bag inside. "Why?"

"Come on, Sid. Agents died. You were there. I saw

the pictures." He grimaced. "In all my years, I've never seen… well, never. Let's just leave it at that. How about we go and get something to eat?"

She crossed her arms. "How about you tell me what's going on? I should be in on this, you know."

"Headquarters is in turmoil at the moment. It almost takes an act of God to keep these incidents out of the papers." Hands stuffed in his pockets, he leaned his shoulder on the car. "When I heard the news, I thought it was you in that bloodbath. I'm glad you're still alive."

"Still?"

"Ah, don't start that." He rolled his eyes. "Quit picking sentences and expressions apart."

"Didn't you teach me that?"

"I don't know." Looking at her with his soft eyes, Ted reminded her of the old actor named Brian Keith from movies she watched with her father. Tough, yet soft in a very manly way. "Probably. Let's get out of this cold and go eat. There's a nice little greasy spoon around the corner."

She pushed her back off the car. "Nice little greasy spoon? I don't think so."

He chuckled and offered his elbow. "Aw, come on. I've never seen anything in there that could bite you."

They made their way out of the parking lot and down the sidewalk, brushing by many passersby.

"Sir, I have to have a part in this. I was there, I brought in AV, and now I'm cut out? It doesn't make any sense."

"The Black Slate doesn't make any sense either. Those files are off the books. I'm trying to make sense of it myself."

"And what have you learned?"

"Huh, well, from what I've gathered, the Slate precedes the FBI." He cleared his throat. "It's a mystery where it came from."

"Wouldn't that make the people on the list really old... like you?"

He laughed.

"And," she continued, "Adam Vaughn didn't seem very old. He seemed little older than me."

"Over time, the list... it changes, I guess. I don't know."

"Well, who keeps the list updated?"

"I don't know that either."

"What do you know?"

He pointed at the sign on the door of a restaurant. The stenciled lettering on the glass door read: The Wayfarer. He opened the door and nodded. "We're here."

The smell of fried food and cooking oil wafted into her nostrils. Soft rock music and the clinking of dishes caught her ear. She stepped inside. "Great." She shivered. "At least it's warm."

"Come on." Ted led her toward the back of the quaint but deteriorating establishment that hadn't changed since the fifties. He stopped at a booth and began speaking to someone.

She couldn't see the person until Ted stepped aside. Her eyes grew. Her heart skipped. It was Smoke.

CHAPTER 26

"**H**ELLO, AGENT SHAW." SMOKE HOISTED a Coke. He wore jeans and a dark sweater under a black leather jacket. His face was clean shaven. "Did you miss me?"

Yes.

"No."

Ted removed his coat, hung it on a hook on the booth, and took a seat opposite Smoke. Just he and Smoke practically filled the booth. "Uh… let me scooch over."

"That's all right." Sid grabbed a chair and dragged it over to the table, closer to Ted's side. She sat down, rested her clasped fingers on the table, and looked at Ted.

"Er, well, I guess we don't need any introductions." Ted took off his cap and placed it on the table. Scratched his head. "A little stuffy in here. Waitress!"

A young man came over in a dirty apron with quaffed brown hair dominating one side of his head. The pen in his hand looked heavy. "Yeah, man."

"Er, double cheeseburger with everything, fries—no, onion rings, and a sweet tea." He eyed Sidney. "And you'll be having?"

"Nothing."

"Mister Smoke?"

"I already ordered."

It better not be pancakes.

The waiter nodded. "Coming up, man."

"All right, man." Ted glared at the waiter's back. "Man. Man. Man. Man. Doesn't anyone say sir anymore?" He looked at Sid. "All right, I'll quit. But if he screws my order up, no tip."

"Sir, can we get down to business?"

"That's my girl. Okay, they still want you on this case. You got AV before, they think you can get him again."

"*It* again," Smoke said.

"Wait a second," Sidney interrupted. "Who wants us on this?"

"One at a time." Ted held up his palm. "First, Sid, I can't tell you that. I'm not really sure myself, but for the interim, I'm your new supervisor."

Unusual, but good.

"Second," Ted said to Smoke, "Adam Vaughn is not an *it*. Some person or persons took him out of there. The evidence confirmed that."

I don't think so.

Smoke sat up. "Did the evidence lead to the discovery of Bigfoot, too? An animal or something like an animal tore through those people like the Tasmanian devil. It wasn't a person."

"Just settle down a moment. Your mission"—he pointed at Sidney and Smoke—"is to find Adam Vaughn. Bring him in. Alive. Find him, and we'll find the fiend that did this to our agents."

"Just us?" she said.

"Yes."

"What about resources? Cars? Weapons? Tactical support? Is Mister Smoke going to be armed or not? And what about his ankle tracker?"

Smoke stuck out his boot. No tracker. With a smile, he said, "All gone."

"Ted, how am I supposed to keep track of him then?"

"You'll just have to work together." He leaned forward. "Ah, food is coming."

The waiter had a tray full of food. Three hamburgers and two chili dogs and plenty of fries. He set a burger and fries down in front of Ted.

Ted's face reddened. His voice darkened as he said, "I said onion rings."

"No man, no, you didn't," the waiter said, setting the other baskets in front of Smoke. "I can get some, man, but it will be extra."

The veins in Ted's neck started to bulge. He glared at the young man.

"No, it won't."

"Take it easy, man. I'll get your rings. Stat." He sauntered off.

Smoke squirted ketchup on his fries and Sidney fought against her giggles.

"What?" Ted said, checking the contents of his burger.

"Nothing," she replied. A giggle erupted.

"All right, now what's so funny?"

"You sounded like Batman," Smoke interjected. Then he imitated. "*I said onion rings.*"

Sidney's face flushed and her giggles continued. She stopped herself. "But it was way better than 'Do you feel lucky, punk?' I thought that was coming."

Ted snatched up his burger and stuffed it into his mouth. "Screw both of you." Ketchup dripped onto his shirt. "Aw, dammit."

Sidney caught a playful look in Smoke's eyes. She felt a spark inside.

Sense of humor a plus. Stuff your face with unknown parts of a swine, minus.

"So, Ted, it's just us then? Again, who is my backup?"

"It's you and him." He swallowed his food. "And me. He reports to you. You report to me. The clock is still ticking on your two weeks. Remember, this is off the books. The less everyone else knows, the better."

Smoke dipped one of his fries in the ketchup. "So there's a mole in the FBI then?"

That's what I was thinking.

"No, there isn't any mole. Just loose lips and big-eared busybodies." Ted tucked a napkin under his chin. "I have enough on my plate without any more probing questions. And so far as I'm concerned, until it's over, the less I know, the better." He bit into his burger.

"Wherever you go, we're going together," she said to Smoke.

"Fine, but that might be a bit awkward when we're sleeping." He leaned closer. "Does that mean I'm staying at your place?"

Sidney's eyes got big. "No, you know what I meant!"

"Ha," Ted laughed. "He turned the tables on you, Sid. I like that."

"I've got everything I need: my own ways," Smoke said, tapping his head, "and my own gear. Just step aside and let me make this happen." He looked straight into her eyes. "I want this murderer as much as you do, and at some point you're going to have to put some trust in me."

Sidney shook her head. "We'll see."

Ted grumbled at the fries in his basket. "Where the heck are my onion rings?"

She glanced back at Smoke. "So, do you have any leads?"

He drained his Coke and clopped the plastic tumbler on the table. "Nope."

CHAPTER 27

"**Y**OU KNOW," SMOKE SAID, RIDING shotgun in the Interceptor, "there's one thing I can't figure."

"About what?" Sidney said.

"AV. If he turned into a werewolf—"

"A werewolf?" *Oh lord, please don't be some Twilight geek.*

"In theory."

"Uh, stupid theory." She pulled the car to a stop at the light. "I think I like the Bigfoot idea better."

"Well, you saw a pack of wolves for yourself. So did I."

"And you thought they were coyotes. Perhaps they were were-coyotes?" The light changed, and she eased on the gas. "That said, I'm not liking your theory. It's ludicrous."

"My point is, AV's clothes were gone. Not a stitch. If he turned into a werewolf or something else, there would have been evidence of something." He pointed up the highway. "Take the next exit."

"So, you're ruling out the supernatural then?" She nodded her head. "Good for you."

"Well—"

"Well, I won't have any of it." She accelerated. "Monsters don't roam Washington."

"Hah, Washington's full of them. They just prefer human form." His head turned right. "Uh, you missed my exit."

Sidney jammed on the brakes and shifted into reverse. She eyed the rearview mirror and gunned the gas.

"Hey," Smoke said, "there's a lot of traffic coming our way. Not a good decision."

"What's the matter, are you afraid I might run over a groovy ghoulie?"

"A what?"

"Nothing." A few car horns blared as they whizzed by. Sidney gunned the Interceptor down the exit ramp. "How much farther?"

"About three miles." He shifted in his seat. "Are you telling me your skin didn't crawl when you stood in the middle of that bloodbath?"

"No, my skin didn't crawl."

"Your friend's head was twisted clean off."

Her throat tightened a little. She thought about Dydeck's family. The funeral. A closed coffin was never a good thing. "I'll let forensics figure that out."

"And I guess you'll read it in the reports you'll never see. Ha." He pointed right. "Turn there."

She hit the blinker and turned right down a blacktopped road marred with low spots and potholes. The car plunged into a pothole and lurched upward.

Smoke stared out the window. "You just lost a cap."

She kept driving.

"Aren't you going back for it?"

"No."

"But that's littering."

"No it isn't."

"Yes—"

She hit the brakes, lunging Smoke forward. Putting the car in reverse, she hit pothole after pothole. Coming to a stop, Sidney put the car in park and got out. Outside, she located the hubcap, picked it up, walked over to Smoke's door, opened it, and dropped it in his lap. She got back in the car again.

"What do you want me to do with this?"

"Shove it."

Smoke flipped it around between his hands. "Usually these old cars are nothing but black rims. It'll probably look better without it anyway." He tossed the cap in the back seat. "Take the next left. Another mile up or so."

Sidney's knuckles were white on the steering wheel. She couldn't shake the image of Dydeck's headless body from her mind. She knew his wife, Jean, and his children, Larry and Zoey. Her heart ached for them.

"Are you all right?" Smoke said.

"Fine."

"This is strange." He cleared his throat. "And I know plenty about strange. I've seen bodies after fifty-caliber bullets ripped through them. At least, I've seen what was left of them. I saw plenty of people decapitated in the desert. It's gruesomely horrible. That said, I've never sensed anything like this before. Eerie."

Goosebumps rose on her arms as she wound the wheel to the left. Sidney couldn't deny the eeriness she felt either, or the sickness the scene stirred inside her.

They passed by some small homes and trailers.

"Next right," Smoke said.

Ahead, an old gas station sign was mounted on a light pole twenty feet in the air. Below it was an old service station, neatly kept. It had two closed garage bays on the left and the store front on the right. The gas pumps were gone, but the overhead canopy remained. It all had been converted into an apartment or house of some sort.

"This is where you live?" she said. The place was almost forty minutes from D.C., east of the Potomac. "Strange place for a gas station."

Smoke popped open his door, but before he got out he said, "It's an old place. Mostly for the locals and family. I picked it up at an estate auction several years ago." He closed the door and headed toward the apartment. "Are you coming?"

Her palms started sweating.

Strange place to be with a strange man.

CHAPTER 28

S HE PICKED UP THE FILE on AV and made her way after him, eyeing the garage bays.

"What's in there?"

"That's where I keep my friends," he said, reaching inside his pocket and producing a set of keys.

"Ah, Fat Sam and Guppy then?"

He tilted his head back and laughed. "You remember! No, but I can't wait to tell them you said that." He stood at the door beside the large block glass window. The heavy grey steel door had both a keypad and a key hole. He stepped in front of her and punched in the code. "I hate carrying keys."

Me too.

Smoke shoved the door open and stepped aside, gesturing. "After you."

Sidney crossed over the threshold. Her heart raced a little.

What is wrong with me?

She took a long draw through her nose. The glass

wall offered little light to an otherwise dim room. It was quiet.

"Hold on." Smoke brushed by her. He stopped at a circuit box and pushed up the black handle. The overhead incandescent lights came on, and the room hummed with life. "That should be better."

A sofa, kitchenette, refrigerator, cupboards, and an island with two stools made for a quaint apartment remarkably similar to her own. An office desk and computer monitors filled one back corner. Two tall dark-green gun safes filled another. It was a lot more modern and cozy than she expected from seeing the outside.

No back door.

"Make yourself comfortable." He sat down and turned on the computer. "As best you can, anyway. It's not much for entertaining. And ignore the cobwebs; I haven't dusted in over a year."

"Ha ha." She took a seat on the sofa, tossed the folder on the coffee table, and opened it up. "So, bounty hunter, you don't have any leads?"

"Nuh-uh." He pecked the keyboard of his computer. "But give it some time and I'll have something."

Adjacent to him, she squinted her eyes toward the monitors. There were four in all. The biggest displayed security camera feeds from outside. Smoke's broad back blocked the front screen from her view. *This is awkward.* She pulled out a picture of Rod Brown, AV's goon.

"Maybe we should check up on Rod Brown."

Smoke stopped typing and swiveled around in his chair to face her.

"I already did."

"What? When?"

"Yesterday, right after they took the leash off." He cocked his head. "You look angry. Are you angry?"

Sidney's nails dug into her palms. She'd been put on ice, but Smoke had been given free range? *Ted's going to get it.* "What did you find?"

"Rod's dead."

She leaned forward. "Dead how? I didn't see anything in the news about it."

"FBI covered it up after I called them. Just like the other one."

Sidney's pulse quickened. Her jaw muscles clenched.

Smoke rose out of his chair and gestured at it. "Have a seat. I'll show you what I discovered."

"Oh, I can't wait to see your big discovery, but I'm fine where I am. Just tell me what you did."

"I went to Rod's apartment, picked the lock, and went inside. His blood was everywhere, just like we saw at Benson. The only difference was Rod's head was... missing." He turned and plucked away at the keyboard. "I took a few pictures of the scene before I called. Can you stomach it?"

She eased her way over and gazed at the monitor. Blood soaked the carpet and was splattered on the walls. Rod's corpse lay headless on the floor. A queasy feeling sank into her stomach and weakened her knees.

"It takes time to get used to it," Smoke said, easing back. "But it's best you don't."

"Did anyone report a disturbance? Screams? Someone must have heard something."

"Growls," he said, taking hold of the mouse.

"I don't think werewolves lock doors."

"Maybe someone else did. Besides"—he clicked on another file—"the residents did report seeing something tall and hairy sprinting through the streets."

"There are such things as bearded runners, you know."

He opened up a video file. "True. But here's a little local footage I hacked into, from the condos."

"You hacked into?"

"Sort of." He pointed at the screen. "Just watch."

The video clip showed a view of the condominium complex's parking lot. It was nighttime, and most of the spaces were filled. The lamp posts illuminated much but not all. A tall figure— distant from the camera angle— glided along the perimeter wall.

Sidney's spine tingled.

The image was unclear, but its shoulders were hulking, and a snout looked to be protruding from its face. It jumped, grasping the high wall's ledge and pulling itself over with ease. Then it vanished. It all happened in a few seconds.

"Go back," she said, "frame by frame."

Smoke toggled the keyboard. The video wound back frame by frame.

"There's something in its hand."

"Yeah, I know," Smoke said, zooming in. It looked like a dripping skull was clutched in a big paw. "I'm pretty sure that's Rod's head."

CHAPTER 29

THE HUMAN BRAIN IS A powerful organ. It can detect the difference between reality and the finest computer-generated images. What Sidney saw wasn't a hoax, but that wasn't the problem. What she saw wasn't human. The limbs were too long. The movements impossibly fluid.

"Maybe a seven-foot-tall ape escaped from the zoo," Smoke said, powering down the monitors. "Or maybe there is a Sasquatch, even though I always figured him to be bigger."

Sidney rubbed her head.

"It's a lot to take in," Smoke said. "I have some aspirin."

"No." She made her way back over to the sofa. "Just give me a moment."

Smoke turned on a TV that hung on the wall. The local news was on.

"You know, it always amazes me how deft the FBI are at covering things up. The sad thing is, I don't think there's enough news time to air all the stories they cover up. And if there were, people would be overwhelmed by the reality of the horrible world we really live in." He sat down on the other end of the sofa and kicked his boots off onto the table. "And in the last few days, I've learned the world is even worse than I thought it was."

"We need to learn what we can about the Drake." She stared at the big screen. "I spent my time poking around the last two days, and I picked up a few things. It's owned by a real estate investor. Aside from the hotel and restaurants, I found almost nothing. There isn't even a website about the barge island on the river."

"Sure, follow the money. I'm sure the IRS has something."

"I made some calls to some friends, and they're pretty tight-lipped right now." She spread some of the file pictures out on the table. "But I did learn the Drake Corporation operates a lot of subsidiary companies. They own most of these locations that Adam Vaughn frequents."

"I think he'll show up."

"Where? Here?" She shook her head. "He's hiding somewhere."

"He's cocky. He'll be out and about."

"We can't stake all of those places out, and they'll be looking for us."

"True, but that's why I have Fat Sam and Guppy on it."

She rolled her eyes and got up. *Damn, I'm still in my gym clothes.* "I'm going. If you can control yourself, stay put and I'll swing by and get you tomorrow." She looked around. "Say, do you have a phone?"

"I have a burner."

"Let me have it." She pulled her phone from her bag. "Here's mine."

They each put themselves in the other's phone as a contact.

"Wow, you just gave me your number and I didn't even ask for it. I'm flattered."

"I'm not."

Her phone buzzed. She grabbed it from him. There was a text from her mother. It read: Allison's gone.

Racing down the road, Sidney pounded on the steering wheel. "I don't need this right now." Her phone rang. "What's going on, Mom?"

"It's been seven hours, Sidney, and we can't find her anywhere." Her mother sobbed. "I'm worried."

"This isn't the first time it's happened," Sid said, accelerating up the highway ramp. "Aren't you used to it?"

"Never, but Megan," Sally's voiced cracked, "it's not fair to Megan. It breaks my heart and makes me so angry. And sad!"

"Did she steal a car? How did she get out of there? You're five miles from anywhere."

There was a silence.

"Mom, you *are* five miles from anywhere, aren't you? The camp, not the house?"

"We thought the house would be a nice change."

Sidney squeezed her phone. Her parents used to be

tough as nails, but over the past few years they'd gotten softer. Almost feeble in many ways.

God, don't let that happen to me.

"Your father and Joe are out looking for her now. I'm sure they'll find her."

No, they won't.

"Mom," Sidney softened her voice, "Allison's going to have to figure this out on her own. You've given her all the love you can. There's nothing more you can do."

Sobbing, her mother said, "You're a good girl, Sid. You know how to say the right things."

"I'm just repeating what you told me."

"Oh!" her mother said, perking up. "I hear the garage door opening." There was a pause. Suddenly, she screamed in the phone. "It's Allison! He's got Allison! She looks okay!" *Click!*

Sidney looked at her phone and said to it, "Are you frickin' kidding me?"

Buzz... Buzz... Buzz...

Sidney stretched her arms through her bedsheets, fingers searching for her phone. Bright morning light peeked in through the apartment's blinds. She found her phone. 8:00 a.m. "Ugh. Already." She'd been in bed by 2:00 am, but it felt like five minutes ago. *Screw it.* She set the snooze and sank back into her bed.

Buzz... Buzz... Buzz...

She forced her heavy eyelids open. Her phone was still clutched in her hand. 8:08 a.m. A crack of sunlight gleamed in her eye. Sidney's bare feet crossed the cold floor to the window, where she pulled the curtains closed. *That's better.* She set the snooze again and crawled back under the sheets. A few things raced through her mind. Smoke. Allison. Megan. Smoke. She drifted off to sleep. She dreamed. Smoke. Fire. Satin sheets.

Knock. Knock. Knock.

She lurched up in bed. A thin film of sweat coated her body. Her phone read 8:13 a.m. *That's odd*, she thought, panting a little. *It shouldn't have gone off yet. Sounded like a knock.* Yawning, she stretched her arms out wide. Normally she was on the move by six, except on the weekends. *I'm not even sure what day it is.*

Knock. Knock. Knock.

Her eyes widened. She grabbed her Glock and headed toward the front door in nothing but a black T-shirt and panties.

She'd been in this apartment a year, but only one time had this door been knocked on—by a couple of college guys who lived a few doors over. It had been an invitation to one of their parties. They never looked her way again after she shoved her badge and an earful of her legal authority in their faces.

Sidney checked the peephole. Smoke stood on the other side, holding a tray of coffee and wearing a pair of sunglasses.

How does he know where I live!

162

CHAPTER 30

"WHAT ARE YOU DOING HERE?" she said through the door.

"I was in the neighborhood and thought I'd bring some coffee over."

A playful thought entered Sidney's mind. She swung the door open.

Smoke's jaw hung in the air.

She plucked a cup of coffee out of the carrier, said "Thank you," and shut the door in his face. From the other side of the door she heard him say, "I thought I'd come over and we could get a jump on things."

"Really, and what kind of things did you want to jump on?" She set down the coffee, headed to her room, grabbed a pair of jeans and a maroon sweater, and slipped them on. She could hear his reply through the door.

"It's not like that."

"You're a man, aren't you?"

There was a pause. "Well, it's kinda like that, but not the way you think. I have a lead."

She buttoned her jeans. "Hold on." Inside the

bathroom she brushed her teeth and clipped her hair up. *No.* Back in the bedroom, she found an FBI-issued ball cap, put it on, and laced up some rubber-soled boots.

"Aren't you going to invite me in?" Smoke said.

And break my last seven months of chastity?

She checked herself in the mirror again and strapped her weapon on. She saw her bed reflecting in the mirror.

Just let him in. Long enough is long enough.

"Hello?" she heard him say. "The biscuits are getting cold."

The biscuits are getting cold? The fires inside her dimmed. *Cheap thrill killed.* She pulled her hat down, grabbed her coffee and bag, and opened the door.

"Don't ever do this again," she said, locking the door behind her, "and you can explain how you found me later." Her stomach growled. "Where's my biscuit?"

"Oh," he said, rubbing his neck. "I was joking about that. I ate on the way over."

She glared at him.

"Nice hat," he said, eyeing the three big letters. "Not exactly discreet considering where we're headed."

"And where might that be?" She scanned the parking lot. "And how did you get here?"

"Automobile." He pointed at the parking lot as they made their way down the stairs. "I can drive too, you know."

"Well, we won't be finding out about that anytime soon." There was an old VW bus, red with a white top, she hadn't seen before. "Please tell me you aren't driving that."

He looked at the bus. "That? No." He pointed to the

space on the other side, where there was a primer-gray Camaro. A mid-eighties IROC version. "Those are my wheels."

"We'll take the Interceptor."

"It's too slow."

"I didn't think we were in a hurry." She headed for her car. The windows were frosted over. The trunk groaned when she opened it up and grabbed the ice scraper. She handed it to Smoke. "Get to work."

"My car's warm and ready. The bucket seats are cozy."

"Please stop." She grabbed her jacket from the back seat and then started up her car. "Hurry up, and then get in."

Scraping, Smoke said, "I have all my gear in my car."

"And I have all my gear in mine." She closed the door and took a sip of coffee. Flipped on the defroster. The fan rattled. Her neck tightened. Smoke's suggestion seemed more promising.

Nah, let him scrape.

Finishing up, Smoke rapped on the window with his knuckle and said with icy breath, "Why don't we take both cars?"

Her nostrils flared. *Screw it.* She shut off the engine, got out of the car, and locked it.

Smoke tossed the scraper in the trunk and started to close it.

"Hold on." She took out a black duffle bag that clattered with metal and swung it over her shoulder. "All right."

Smoke clamped the lid down, headed for his car, and opened up the passenger side door.

"This isn't a date." She placed her bag in the back seat.

"No, it's common courtesy."

Sidney took her seat and Smoke closed the door. Seconds later, they were roaring down the road. The Camaro's acceleration pinned her to her seat. It had a roll cage inside, and the dash rattled and squeaked. Smoke filled up his racing seat. His head almost touched the ceiling.

"I appreciate you letting me drive," Smoke said over the hum of the engine. "That's one thing I hate about prison. I don't get to drive anywhere."

"Don't get used to it. We have a stop to make."

"Stop, why?"

"Take the next left, a right and then another left."

"Sure, where are we going?"

"Just do it." *Turn about is fair play.*

She took the lid off her coffee and took another drink. Smoke was being extremely cooperative for a man who had problems with authority. He was up to something. His behavior was way outside of his profile. Smoke made the second left.

"Turn here."

They entered a facility full of orange-doored storage garages. He pulled his car to a stop at the key pad. "Uh…"

"Seven six seven five."

He punched it in, and the gate glided open.

"Straight back and to the right."

Smoke cruised toward the back, where cars, boats, and RVs were parked in rows. He pulled into an open slot.

She picked up her belongings, got out, and said, "Wait here."

"Can I at least get out?"

"Sure."

A few minutes later she pulled out in a Dodge Challenger Hellcat: phantom black, with flame-orange stripes on the hood and pinstripes on the side. She pushed on the gas, unleashing a throaty exhaust note.

Smoke took off his glasses. Brows up and eyes wide, he strolled over.

"I think I'm in love."

"With me, or the car?"

"Heh... I'll get my stuff."

CHAPTER 31

CRUISING DOWN THE HIGHWAY, SMOKE ran his
fingers over the dash. "Seven hundred and seven
horsepower, the most powerful production engine."
He bobbed his chin. "Now that's something. I read about
these in prison. Pretty new. How'd you come by it?"

"Police auction," she said, fingers hugging the heated
steering wheel. *I've missed my baby.* "I outbid a lot of
interested people. Pissed off many men."

"I bet."

"It came down to me and Ted." She plucked her
shades from the console and put them on. "At the end of
the day it was my Hellcat, not his."

Glasses off, Smoke inspected everything. "He missed
out. So why the attraction?"

"Love cars. Love the name. My dad actually had some
comics with a superhero named Hellcat I kind of liked."
Too much information, Sid.

Smoke smiled. "Ah, very interesting."

"Not to mention the rear-wheel drive and all the
awesome power. It's sort of a given."

"So, was this a drug runner's car?"

"Snagged north of the Arizona border. The auction was in Texas. I drove him all the way home."

"I thought cars were *hers?*"

"Does he look like a *her*?"

He shook his head no.

"I'm heading south, you know," she said. "Unless there's another direction I should be going."

"Right, right. No, south is good." He poked at the GPS. "Do you mind?"

"It would help to know where I'm going." She checked the speedometer. It read ninety. The feel of the road, the sound of the engine, she lost herself in it. She eased off the gas and set the cruise control at seventy. "So tell me about this lead. How did you get it?"

"Fat Sam—"

"And Guppy. Sheesh, I should have known." She switched lanes. "I'm wondering if they're even real."

"Oh, they're real, but it's important that I keep my resources secret." He finished tapping on the GPS. "There we go."

"What is that?"

"Mitchell-Bates Hospital. Closed as of 2004. One hundred and seventy-five beds. Three floors and a basement." He took a drink of coffee. "Two miles from the highway. Once public and now private property."

"And who owns it now?"

"A real estate developer, which is a subsidiary of..."

"The Drake Corporation."

"Actually, Drake Incorporated. We checked at the Secretary of State's office, which wasn't easy seeing how three states are in the immediate area."

"So there are lots of companies, different names and doing business as?"

"Yep." He nodded. "And no real names."

"And I guess they all pay their taxes."

"Do you want me to find out?"

"No." Sidney had done her share of white-collar investigations. Digging through layer after layer of false names and companies was interesting. The top lawyers and accountants dotted every 'i' and crossed every 't' on the good ones. In the most thorough cases it took an act of God to bring them down, and that was only after years were exhausted in the court systems that the enemy knew too well. *This is a lot deeper than just one man.*

"Shadow companies like the Drake probably benefit from a few congressmen and senators in their pockets."

She thought of Congressman Wilhelm and the last words he had said: "Watch your step."

Things were quiet the next ninety minutes of driving, and then she took the Grandview Road exit. A pair of steel-crafted yellow swing gates barred the road that led into the parking lot.

"Looks like we walk from here."

"I'm not leaving my car out here," Sidney said. She got out and made her way to the gates. A heavy padlock down inside a steel mesh cage held the gates together. She scanned the area. The Mitchell-Bates Hospital sign was in disrepair. No cameras were mounted on the light poles leading to the entrance. Only the sound of highway traffic caught her ears. She drew her weapon, shot the lock off, swung the gate open, and got back in the car.

"Subtle," Smoke said.

She put the car in drive. "Let's get this over with."

CHAPTER 32

"MAYBE HE IS, MAYBE HE isn't in here," she said, driving forward. "Perhaps Fat Sam and Guppy are wrong."

"They aren't wrong."

"Maybe there's another way out."

Smoke shrugged.

As they rolled up the road between the tall trees, the rising sun dimmed behind misty clouds. The brisk wind stirred the leaves on the parking lot as they approached. The small brick hospital stood in a woodland of falling leaves and pines. Not a car was in the lot. Patches of tall grass popped up through the blacktop.

"He's in here, huh?" she said to Smoke. "It looks pretty abandoned to me."

"It's a lead," he said. "Besides, looks can be deceiving. There's another side to the building, you know." He shook his head. "Man, this is the worst recon ever."

"What's that supposed to mean?" she said, reaching into the back seat for her gym bag. She took out another shoulder holster. A Kevlar vest. Another Glock was ready, along with two fifteen-round magazines. She slipped off her jacket, put on the Kevlar vest, and put the jacket over it. "I don't think there's that much to recon."

"Then why are you gearing up like that?"

"Because I don't normally get to." She pulled the car under the canopy that led to the emergency room entrance, opened her door, and dropped a foot outside. "Are you coming or not?"

"Pop the trunk."

She followed him to the back of the car, where he opened his oversized gym bag. He put on his own Kevlar vest and strapped a pair of 9mm Beretta pistols to his hips. He finished by stuffing a single-action army sheriff's pistol in the back of his pants.

"A revolver?" she said.

"It's sentimental."

"All right, cowboy." As she turned toward the hospital entrance, something caught her eyes. She froze.

A white-grey wolf stood twenty feet away, teeth bared. Its muscular back was more than waist tall. It was one of the biggest canines she'd ever seen.

"Uh, Smoke?"

"Yeah?" he said, turning. "Oh... that's one big dog."

Sidney's back tightened. Her fingertips tingled. She knew dogs but not wolves. They were wild. Ferocious. She reached for her weapon.

Before she could even touch it, the wolf had snarled and sprinted away.

Sidney jumped when Smoke closed the trunk.

He had a tire iron in his hand. "Let's go catch that werewolf."

"I think it will be a few more hours before any of them come out." She took the tire iron from his hand and made her way onto the landing. A set of sliding glass doors were closed, and the side entrance steel door was locked. She wedged the tire iron in between the doors and started to pry. The doors cracked open an inch. "A little help," she grunted.

Smoke gripped the door's edge and gave a powerful tug. The doors split apart another foot. Straining, he said, "Think you can fit?"

"Ha," she said, squeezing through. Smoke forced himself inside, and the doors sealed shut with the tire iron outside. "Ew," she said, covering her nose. "It smells like the dead in here."

Inside, the lighting was dim other than the natural light from the windows.

"Do you hear that?" Smoke said, tilting his head. The sound of electricity hummed inside the walls. "Something is going on in here." He started forward, shuffling by the old waiting room chairs and into the ER. There were several gurneys with rotting curtains hanging around them. "What do you think? Follow the smell?"

Sidney remained behind Smoke's shoulder and followed him into the central hall, plugging her nose. *This is disgusting.* The long hallway was darker because the patient room doors were closed, blocking the sunlight. Smoke stopped at one of them and pushed it open. It groaned on the hinges and swung inward. *Is he visiting somebody?*

It was a two-patient room with soiled linens rotting on the beds. The air was musty, rotten, and stale.

Sidney coughed. "Do you have a thing for bad smells?"

Smoke glided to the window and stood where the daylight crept in through the blinds. He pulled them aside with two fingers. "We aren't alone."

Sidney took a look. Smoke was right. More cars were parked behind the building: two navy-blue cargo vans and several dark sedans. A box truck was backed into the service drive. All of it was shadowed by the tall trees that snuffed out the bright rising light.

She glanced up at Smoke. "I can't say I'm glad that you're right. Come on."

"I'd be disappointed if I was wrong."

Heading out of the room, she came to a stop. Footsteps and the shuffle of feet came from the room above. The steps creaked and were moving down the hall. Sidney followed the sound down toward the emergency exits. Smoke was a large shadow behind her. The doors were closed at the stairwell, but she heard the latch of the doors above pop open. She slid to one side of the doors, and Smoke took the other. Her heart thumped in her chest.

After about thirty seconds, Smoke shrugged. "They either went up or went back." He popped the door open and peered inside the dark stairwell. "Huh, there's a basement too. I have a coin. Heads we go up, tails we go—*ulp*!"

A hand shot out and pulled Smoke into the stairwell. The door slammed shut behind him.

CHAPTER 33

"**S**MOKE!"

Sidney shoved on the door, but there was no give. Something blocked the other side. She thrust her shoulder into it. It cracked open and slammed shut. She could hear the scuffle of a fight on the other side. A man screamed.

"Smoke!"

Wham!

A heavy body rocked the door. She heard the heavy blows of bone on bone and flesh on flesh. Hard smacks. Kicking. Punching. Wrestling. She found her flashlight and shone it through the rectangular portal. A bloodshot eye blinked in the light. The face was scarred. Subhuman. She tapped the nose of her gun on the glass.

"Back off!"

The face ducked away.

She lowered her shoulder, rammed into the door, and winced. No give. She wanted to shoot. Blast away, but Smoke was over there, fighting for his life.

Come on! Come on! Think, Sid! Think!

"Back away, Sid," Smoke roared from the other side. "Back away!"

Sidney stepped aside. The door flung inward. Smoke appeared, dragging another man in a headlock.

"Stay away from the door," Smoke warned. The door clasped shut. Footsteps scurried up the stairwell. "Stay here." Smoke wrestled the struggling man to the floor and wrenched the man's arm behind his back. *Pop!* The shoulder was dislocated, but the man didn't cry out.

"What are you doing?" Sidney said.

Chest heaving, Smoke replied, "I'm immobilizing him." He wrenched the man's other arm. *Pop.* The other shoulder gave.

Sidney's stomach turned.

The man-like thing thrashed with purpose, arms hanging limp as noodles from the sockets. Its face was ghoulish and veiny. It gathered itself on its feet.

Smoke swept the legs out from under it.

It crashed back-first to the floor.

Smoke pinned it and jammed his gun barrel in its chest.

"Don't kill him," Sidney ordered.

"I hit him with everything I had. He didn't even grunt."

"That's not a license to kill."

"You're just going to have to trust me on this, Agent Shaw." He squeezed the trigger.

Ka-blam!

The man-like thing lurched up and smacked Smoke in the chin.

He staggered back.

It started walking down the hall, arms dangling at its sides with a hole clean through its back and chest.

Sidney took aim.

Blam! Blam! Blam!

It tumbled over with its kneecap blasted apart.

"Good shot." Smoke wiped his brow and headed after their fallen attacker where it writhed on the floor. "I think it's a zombie." He pointed his weapon at its head.

Blam!

"Zombies aren't real," she said, catching her breath and holstering her gun.

"I don't know," Smoke replied.

She kneeled down. Whoever or whatever the man was, it didn't bleed: it oozed. It still moved. Her skin turned clammy. "This is sick."

"Good thing we're in a hospital."

Sidney eyed him. "How many were in there?"

"Just two. One I think was a man. I kicked him solid in the balls." He cracked his neck. "That's when I dragged this fiend out of there. Do you think it's that captain?" he said, referring to the man driving AV's boat she'd mentioned earlier.

"No, but his skin is just like what I saw." She took out her phone. "No signal."

"No surprise." He tipped his head toward the stairwell. "How about I scout it out?"

"How about we scout it out? But another approach would be better, seeing how they know we're here." She made her way into another patient room and peered out through the window. None of the cars had moved. "Doesn't look like we scared anyone off, either."

"Not yet," Smoke said, leaning on the door frame. "But I say we take it to them."

If AV was here, then he certainly knew they were here. It might take hours to clear the building, not to mention the unnatural elements that surrounded them. What kind of man had they just taken down? It had attacked, but it hadn't tried to eat them.

It's not a zombie. There's no such thing as zombies. She headed back into the hall. The man-like thing on the floor was still moving.

"Strange," Smoke said, looking down at it. "I thought the head wound would kill it."

"This isn't a movie. This is reality."

Smoke switched weapons. "And this is a forty-five automatic loaded with hollow points." He pointed at the writhing thing's heart.

Blam.

It stopped moving.

He blew the smoke rolling from the barrel. "Critical hit."

Irritated, she said, "Will you stop shooting?"

"We needed to know how to take these things out, and now we do."

"A bullet in the heart does that to anything." She made her way back down the hallway, stopping and listening at patient doors from time to time. On the other side of the hall, Smoke did the same. She traversed the hall, passing the elevators. She heard a ding and turned back.

Smoke stood in front of the elevators. The up button glowed with light. The doors split open and he half-stepped inside. He looked at her and said, "Going up?"

"I'm not taking the elevator." She crept in halfway and pressed buttons two and three, grabbed Smoke's arm, and pushed him out. She ran down the hall with Smoke on her heels. Flashlight ready, she entered the stairwell, jogged up the steps, and stopped on the second floor landing. She peered through the door's portal. Figures crowded in front of the elevator down the hall. One of them was limping.

"That's the guy," Smoke said, cocking his pistol. "It has to be."

Sidney counted four men, but she didn't see any weapons. It was odd. One of them disappeared into the elevator. Necks craned forward until the man stepped out into view again. Voices mumbled among themselves, and the group spread out, vanishing into patient rooms and behind the nurse's station.

"Ambush," she whispered to Smoke.

"I say we start at the top and work our way down. Give them something to think about."

"Agreed." She turned her flashlight up the stairwell and took it two steps at a time. She stopped halfway to the first landing. A man stood there in ragged clothes, hollow-eyed and ugly. He held a grenade-sized object in his hands.

"FBI! Hands up!"

The man's thoughtless expression didn't change as he dropped the grenade down the stairwell. It bounced off the first step.

Smoke scooped it up. "Stun grenade." He flung it back at the man.

Sidney squeezed her eyes shut and covered her ears.

Flash! Boom!

The sound inside the stairwell rocked her senses. She saw dizzying spots and sagged down the steps. There was ringing, ringing and ringing, and everything faded to black.

CHAPTER 34

A SPLASH OF COLD WATER SNAPPED Sidney out of her sleep. Wide-eyed and head aching, she tried to spit the gag from her mouth. Something bit into her wrists, which were tied behind her back. Her feet were bound as well.

"Huh, huh," a man said, lumbering by with a plastic bucket in his hands. He was thickset and bald. He wore a heavy blue sweater, grey sweatpants, and white tennis shoes. He poured the bucket of water on Smoke, who sat on the floor by her side, bound the same way.

Smoke coughed and sputtered.

The man walked away and disappeared through a double doorway.

Spitting the gag from his mouth, Smoke said, "You all right?"

Sidney nodded. Other than a piercing headache and stiff limbs, she was fine. They looked to be in the basement cafeteria, judging by the checkered tiles on the floor. They weren't alone, either. Below the incandescent lights were more people, working at tables. They wore masks, gloves, and dark-grey scrubs. Some sat at the tables and others stood. She didn't have a clear view of what they were doing. Not a one glanced their way.

"See that?" Smoke said in a low tone. Two goons in pea coats lorded over a lone table. It had their guns and gear on it. "Be patient."

It was easier said than done. Sidney had never been captured before. Never been a captive of any sort. The revolting smells didn't help, either. She strained against her bonds. Her eyes watered.

"Save your energy," Smoke advised.

Balled up, she let her body go slack. Smoke was right. She focused on what the others were doing. A small figure that looked to be a boy taped up a box the others had loaded and moved it to a stack in the corner. *Hmmm.* Five people in all were making packages of some sort. It reminded her of the scene at Sting Ray's bar. Children being exploited. She clenched her teeth.

A small bell rang. The workers stopped what they were doing, and without a glance among them they departed from the room.

With great effort, she spat the gag from her mouth and gasped.

"Feel better?" Smoke said.

"No. Hey!" she yelled over at the guards. "I'm a federal agent. I demand to know who is in charge."

The men remained frozen in place without a glance her way. Each one had a shotgun strapped over his shoulder.

She heard Smoke's belly grumble. "I don't think they're serving pancakes."

"No," Smoke said just as the set of doors that led into the hallway opened. Two ghoulish men with clammy skin, wearing denim overalls, walked in. "And I don't think they're here to take our order."

The men came toward them with strong stiff movements. The first one grabbed Smoke by the collar and heaved him up on his shoulder. The second one did the same to Sidney. Draped over the ghastly men's shoulders, they exited the room into a dark hallway and entered another. Sidney's goon set her down in a padded office chair. An antique walnut desk in a well-furnished office was in front of her.

Behind it sat AV in a high-backed leather chair.

His eerie henchmen moved to either side of him.

"I have to admit," AV said, filing his nails, "This is a surprise. I normally fetch my enemies myself. But in this case, you came straight to me." He wore a dark-purple dress shirt with rolled-up sleeves, revealing his hairy arms. The glow of two floor lamps against the back wall brought out the sheen in his waves of jet-black hair. He seemed small between his goons. "Agent Shaw, didn't I mention that I would kill you?"

"Yes, I recall you threatening a federal agent."

AV laughed. "And yet, here you are." He waggled his finger at her. "Did you not see the bodies of your friends? Were they not torn to shreds?"

A coldness overcame her.

"Ah," He continued, "you look confused. He eased back in the chair and rocked a little. "Let me fill you in." He licked his teeth. "I'm a werewolf."

Sidney laughed despite the truth behind his words and

the tingling that shot up her limbs. "Congratulations," she said. "That must explain the fleas."

"Good one," Smoke said with a nod. "And I told you so."

AV picked up a pistol that lay on the desk. It was Smoke's Colt .45, black matte and pearl-handled, sheriff's model. He popped open the chamber and emptied the bullets out of the cylinder. They were silver. "Either you're a fan of the Lone Ranger, or you are as stupid as most men are."

"Really?" Sidney said, looking over at Smoke. "He's not a werewolf."

"Ah, a skeptic. I love a skeptic." AV opened a drawer and pulled a knife out. The wavy blade looked ancient. He turned in his chair and grabbed the hand of one of his goons and placed it on the desk. He skinned the hair off its arm. "Sharp, isn't it?" The knife bit deeper, and he peeled off the skin, exposing the muscle beneath it.

Sidney's skin crawled.

"See, he doesn't even scream." The listless goon leaned back into attention. AV stuck the knife in its thigh. "And he makes for an excellent knife holder." His dangerous eyes narrowed on Sidney. "Can you explain that, Agent Shaw?"

No.

"We call them deaders."

We?

"Cursed flesh brought to life. Flesh automatons made for our bidding. Capable of executing simple commands. Fetch. Fight. Kill."

"That's quite an accomplishment," she said, twisting

her wrists behind her. *I need to get out of here.* "Do you have a patent on it?"

"Humph," he said, plucking a pen from its holder and writing on something. "How did you find me? I need to tie up that loose end."

"It wasn't that hard," Smoke said. "Those wild wolf dogs led us here."

"I don't think so," AV said. "But no matter. I'll figure it out soon enough."

"So, who is 'we'?" she said, turning her ear to him. *Keep him talking.* "I can use all the leads I can get, because you're only the first guy, I mean werewolf, on my list."

"Your tongue is sharp, Agent." He leered at her. "I'm reconsidering."

"Reconsidering what?"

"Twisting your head off first." He picked up a phone that looked to be hers. "You have family, don't you?" He turned her phone toward her. A picture of Megan, her niece, appeared.

How'd he get in there?

"You've seen what I can do," he continued. "Imagine what I could do to her."

The blood rushed through her temples. Her heart sank. *No!*

"Of course, that would be merciful," AV said, flipping through the pictures. "Maybe I'll have her turned into a deader."

"I'm going to kill you," Sidney replied.

"No, Agent Shaw, I am going to kill you." He rose from his chair, pushing it back, and stretched out his arms. "Both of you. I've been waiting to wake you for hours."

He cracked his neck from side to side. "Nighttime is my time." He crushed her phone in his fist and dropped the remains on the desk.

"Told you he was strong," Smoke said, straining at his bonds.

Sidney's heart quickened. *What is happening?!*

AV started to change. His body stretched and convulsed. Coarse hairs sprouted from his face and arms. Muscle bulged and bone groaned. His purple shirt split at the seams. A short snout protruded from his jaws, and his head stretched toward the ceiling. In seconds, AV went from a man to a full-blown werewolf. Evil and lust lurked behind the yellow eyes that rested on Sidney.

Horrified, she sagged in her seat and turned her head away.

This isn't real! This isn't real! This isn't real!

CHAPTER 35

"WHAT'S THE MATTER?" AV SAID, his voice now something monstrous—throaty and raw. "Has your sharp tongue dulled?"

Sidney had seen horrible things, both in real life and in the movies, but nothing compared to the supernatural transformation she'd just witnessed. It was unnatural. Evil. Yet somehow... alluring? Utterly afraid, she pulled her knees up into her chest.

"That's what I like to see," AV said, coming from around the desk. "The brave woman turned into a little girl again." He leaned over her. "Your fear feeds my craving."

She felt his hot breath on her neck. Now she couldn't deny there was something seductive and powerful about it. Her iron will started to cave.

"Yes, yes, Agent Shaw. Give yourself away." He brushed her hair aside with his clawed finger and turned her chin toward him. "Experience every pleasure I can offer that needs awakening in the dark corners of your soul."

He ran his claw down her face, over her chest, and rested his powerful hand on her thigh and squeezed.

She moaned. Dark fires ignited within. She was powerless in the clutch of the uber-man before her.

"Maybe I'll keep you around after all." He ran his finger down her thigh. With his claw, he sliced the cord that bound her ankles. He twisted her around and cut the bonds from her wrists.

Her shoulders sagged. Her body was loose. Languid.

He eased her legs apart. "It's been quite some time, hasn't it, woman?"

Lost in his power, her head fell over on her shoulder. She wanted him. She loathed him. Her eyes found Smoke's. He had a fierce look about him. Seeing the sweat bead on his forehead, a glimmer of her senses returned. AV took her chin and turned it away.

"Don't worry about him—he's a dead man, but you might have a promising future ahead."

"Sidney! Close your eyes! Think of pancakes and butterflies."

What kind of man says that?

"Deaders, kill that fool!" AV ordered. "Feed his corpse to the wolves. I'll be needing Agent Shaw all to myself."

Pancakes and butterflies? The flames of passion turned to angry fires. *Pancakes and butterflies!* She kicked AV's groin with all her force.

He slammed back into the desk.

"Fool woman!" He lurched forward and backhanded her in the face, spinning her like a top from the chair so that she tumbled over.

Her head rang, and all she saw was bright spots and stars.

AV put his big paw on her head and tugged her up to her toes by the hair. "I'm not big on second chances, Pretty."

A clamor rose. Smoke, somehow free of his bonds, wrestled against the clutches of the deaders.

"Excuse me," AV said a moment before he slung Sidney into the wall.

She smacked into it hard and sagged to the floor. Groaning, she forced herself up to her knees and spat blood.

"Run, Sidney!" Smoke urged. "Run!" He slipped away from the deaders only to find himself cornered by AV. The werewolf sneered down on him. Smoke punched him in the throat and poked him in the eye.

AV roared. His claws slashed out.

Smoke twisted away, ducked, and popped up with a knife in his hand. It was the ancient blade that AV had planted in the deader. He cut into the monster's slashing arms, spun under a powerful blow, and drove the blade home into AV's abdomen.

The werewolf staggered back against the wall.

"No! No!" AV cried. "You stabbed me with the Blade of Hoknar. Darkness falls. Darkness falls." He slumped back against the wall, and his eyes began to close.

Sidney got up and wiped the blood from her mouth. "That was close."

Smoke skipped away from the deaders, who wandered the room but didn't attack.

Laughter rumbled in AV's throat, and his mighty

190

form rose again. He plucked the blade from his stomach and showed a mouthful of sharp teeth.

"Fools." He hurled the blade at Smoke.

The big man plucked it out of the air, spun, and buried it hilt-deep in the heart of a deader. He ripped it out and said, "Sid, get out of here!"

"Oh please," AV said, "no one has ever escaped alive." He wiped the saliva dripping from his fangs off of his chin. "I just need to decide which one of you to kill first." He chomped his teeth. "Deader, kill her. I shall kill him." AV sprang from one side of the room to the other. His heavy frame drove the evading Smoke to the ground. His fists came down with speed and power.

Sidney ran for the door.

The dead man cut into her path. Fingers clutched at her waist and tore a belt loop off her pants.

She slugged it in the face.

It leered back into her eyes. Soulless. Empty. Its grabby hand locked around her wrist and slung her to the floor.

She hit hard. "Ugh!"

The deader held her in a fierce grip and pummeled her with its free fist. The hammering blows rocked her body.

She kept her shoulder up to absorb what she could and kicked her hardest with her legs. Her heel connected with its jaw.

"Nuh!" it said, sounding almost human.

With an angry shout, Sidney twisted her wrist free and was on her feet again.

The werewolf had Smoke pinned to the wall by the

neck. Smoke's shaky hand was pointing at the desk. The gun. The bullets. Silver nodules caught her eye. She snatched the old wheel gun up. Strong hands grabbed her feet and jerked her to the floor.

"Ulp!"

Crack!

Her head bounced off the edge of the hardwood desk. She saw red.

"No!"

She kicked it in the face.

"No!"

Her heel crushed its nose in.

"NO!"

She ripped her foot out of its grip and scrambled away on all fours. The other deader lay still, with a knife stuck in its chest. She ripped it out and turned just as the deader dove on top of her. She drove the blade into its chest and pushed it off her.

Smoke!

She pushed off the floor. Smoke held on for his life against the werewolf. Sidney plucked a bullet from the desk and loaded it into the chamber. She cocked back the hammer. "Let him go, AV!"

The wolfman froze with the battered Smoke held tightly in his grip and said, "You don't really think that will work, do you?"

"Only one way to find out."

"Aren't you here to arrest me? After all, I'm no good to your handlers if I'm dead. They need the knowledge within this body."

"Shoot him," Smoke spat out from busted lips. "Shoot him now."

"Let him down," she warned. The adrenaline cleared her mind. She felt in control again.

"Certainly," AV replied, lowering Smoke's busted frame to the ground. "But I don't think you have strong enough cuffs to hold me. Remember what happened the last time. And another thing, silver bullets don't really kill werewolves."

"Then why are you doing what I say?"

"Because I enjoy the game." In a flash, he rocketed by the desk toward the office door.

Sidney fired. *Blam!*

The wolfman burst through the door with a wounded howl and vanished into the hall.

Sidney peeked down both ways. AV the werewolf was gone.

CHAPTER 36

"THAT WAS FAST," SIDNEY SAID, rushing over to Smoke. She helped him to his feet. His hair was matted in blood, and his face was swelling. His Kevlar vest was all torn up. "Are you going to make it?"

He straightened up. "I had my doubts." With a bloody hand, he picked up the other bullets from the table. "Why didn't you shoot him?"

"They want him alive."

"They? Don't let your overzealous sense of duty get me or you killed, Agent Shaw. " He stepped past her and plucked the knife out of the deader's chest. He flipped it around and faced her. "He's a murderer. And murderers must die." He pointed his finger in her face. "I told you he was a werewolf. Now hand over the gun."

"No." She held out her hand. "Hand over the bullets."

"It's my gun."

"I'm not arguing with a twelve-year-old."

Smoke's face drew tight as he handed over the bullets. "Fine. Just, the next time you hesitate, remember—he twists people's heads off!" He made his way into the hall and knelt down by some blood drops on the floor. "Seems you clipped him, and my guess is he didn't like it."

"Follow the blood," she said, loading the bullets into their cylinders. As she made her way down the hall toward the cafeteria, one of the double doors squeaked open. Smoke darted in front of her. A shotgun blast rang out. She flattened on the floor. Aimed her weapon.

In a burst of motion, Smoke jerked one of the peacoat men through the door and ripped the shotgun from his grasp. He lowered the barrel to between the man's eyes.

"No, no man! Please, don't shoot me."

Smoke kneeled down, pressing the barrel deeper into the man's face. "Where's Mister Vaughn?"

"Who?"

Smoke punched him in the gut. "The werewolf."

"Aw man, aw man, I don't know!"

"How many others?" Sidney piped in.

"Just me. Just me."

"Liar," Sidney said, backing into the cafeteria. There were no signs of anybody anywhere.

Pop! Pop! Pop! Pop! Pop!

Bullets ripped through the air from the other end of the hall.

Smoke dragged the man into the cafeteria.

"Who was that?"

"The other man, Allen. Like me, he stayed to finish you off." He chuckled. "And if he doesn't, the others will."

Smoke looked up at Sid. "We've got to go. Time's wasting."

Pop! Pop! Pop! Pop! Pop!

"Yer gonna get wasted, all right," the goon said.

Smoke took the shotgun stock and clocked the goon in the jaw. "I hate big talkers." He nodded at the table. "Get the gear. I'll cover the hall."

Sidney moved, picking up pistols and holsters.

Ka-Blam! Ka-Blam!

She whipped around. Smoke was gone. "Dammit."

He reappeared back inside the door with another shotgun strapped on his shoulder. "Got him."

She took a moment and caught her breath. *Is this really going on? Werewolves and zombie-like men called deaders?* She swooned a little.

Smoke wrapped his arms around her waist and steadied her. "We aren't finished yet. And I think you're going to have quite a shiner, but I can live with it."

"Look who's talking," she said.

Smoke's clothes were blood-soaked in some parts.

The cafeteria suddenly became quiet. She remembered what AV had said: no one ever left alive. She took a shotgun from Smoke's shoulder and pumped the handle.

"Until today."

"Until what today?"

"Nothing," she said, looking at the floor. She found AV's blood. "Let's go."

The blood trail led into the darkness of the stairwell. She turned on her flashlight.

Smoke cut in front of her. "You shine. I'll lead." He

took off up the steps, clearing the first floor and heading up the second flight. He cracked the door open.

Pop! Pop! Pop! Pop!

Bullets blasted into the stairwell doors.

"Turn off the light and cover me," Smoke said.

"Wait."

He surged through the door.

Sidney laid down shotgun cover fire into the middle of the hall. Shots cracked out from everywhere. Muzzle flashes flared. Shielded behind the door, she cracked off a few more rounds and everything fell silent. Now that it was night, the hallway was almost pitch black. The seconds seemed like minutes as she peered into the shadows.

Pop!

A man cried out. A group of shadows tussled in the hall. Something cracked. Another man screamed.

Blam! Blam!

"It's clear," Smoke said, his voice hollow in the blackness of the hall. "Come on. There's still a trail of blood."

Just as Sidney eased into the hallway, the fine hairs on her neck rose. She started to turn. A hairy paw clamped down on her shoulder and dug its sharp nails into her skin.

"I'll take this," the soft savage voice of the wolfman said, sliding Smoke's pistol with the silver bullets out of the back of her pants. "Set down your weapons and stop resisting. You don't know what you're missing."

Hot saliva dripped onto her neck, arousing her carnal

senses. Compelled to obey, she set the shotgun and pistol down.

"I'm not so bad, Pretty," AV said, wrapping his powerful arm around her waist. He picked her up off her feet like a child. "Come quietly now and everything will be fine."

She wanted to believe him. Her rigid body slackened. "No," she managed to say.

"Yes," he replied, moving down into the stairwell's blackness.

In a twisted moment of fate, her terror turned to attraction as she felt herself being carried over the threshold of wickedness. Everything she knew to be right suddenly turned wrong. Reaching deep inside, she found a spark and tried to cry out against her captivating bonds.

AV clamped his hand over her mouth. "Sssh..."

CHAPTER 37

THE SECOND-FLOOR DOORS TO THE stairwell flung open, and Smoke emerged. He hurled himself down the stairwell, crashing into Sidney and AV. The jolt knocked her loose from the werewolf's clutches.

"Fool!" AV roared, lashing out and striking Smoke in the chest.

The hardened soldier crashed into the wall. The stairwell lit up with bright barrel flashes.

Ka-Blam! Ka-Blam! Ka-Blam!

Smoke unloaded his shotgun into AV's chest, rocking the werewolf backward.

Click.

"You're a dead man!" AV roared.

Sidney crawled through the darkness as she heard heavy blows smacking into flesh. Man and monster cursed and snarled. *I have to help!* A clatter of metal skidded over the landing. She dove toward it and felt the cool pistol clutched in her fingers.

Whap! Whap! Whap!

Punches and angry howls filled the stairwell. The

heavy scuffles and grunts were inseparable. Weapon ready, she rushed into the fray, grabbed a handful of coarse hair, and fired.

Blam!

A shrieking howl split her ears, and a swipe of claws knocked her from her feet. She fired again at the sound of feet fleeing up the stairs.

Blam!

Smoke grabbed her hand and moaned, "Stop! Only three more bullets left."

They helped each other to their feet. Smoke leaned on her, limping down the stairwell. He looked like he had crawled out of a mine field.

"We need to get you help."

He spat blood. "I'm fine."

"You don't look fine."

"Well, I look better than most guys who've slugged it out with a werewolf." He groaned. "We need to kill this guy."

"We need more help."

"Follow the blood. I think we've almost got him." He pointed at bloody footprints on the floor. "Staggered. You got him good."

The blood trail led to the emergency room and then to the door of a locked office. She peered through the portal. AV sat in a chair, digging medical pliers into an abdominal wound. He plucked out a bloody silver bullet and tossed it to the floor.

Sidney tapped on the glass and pointed the barrel at him.

The werewolf's eyes widened.

She fired.

Blam!

Cat-quick, he sprang away, crashing through the window and into the parking lot.

"Missed. Dammit!"

Smoke busted the door handle off with a fire extinguisher and kicked it open.

"True, but I think you scared him off," Smoke said, stepping inside and looking out the broken window. "And the hunt starts all over."

"Did you hear that?" she said.

An engine flared up with a gentle roar. A second later, a maroon Cadillac Escalade sped through the parking lot. AV the werewolf filled the seat.

"You've got to be kidding me." She took aim. Smoke pushed the barrel down.

"I think the Hellcat has a better chance of not missing."

She took off, racing into the ER waiting room. The sliding glass doors were sealed and the main entrance door wouldn't open.

Smoke picked up a row of seats and hurled them through the glass. "After you," he said.

Sidney jumped down the steps and flung open the car door.

Smoke slid over the hood.

"Don't you ever do that again!" she said, firing up the engine. She shifted into reverse, hit the gas, and swung the car around. Dropping the car into drive, she stomped on the gas, smoking the wheels.

"Nothing like the smell of burning rubber in the

evening," Smoke said, crawling into the back seat. "Sorry about the upholstery."

"What are you doing?" she yelled at the rearview mirror.

Smoke popped down the rear seat, pulled his duffle bag from the trunk, and crawled back into the front seat. "Getting this," he said, holding an M-16 assault rifle with an M203 grenade launcher mounted under the barrel. "A real beauty, isn't it?"

"Illegal as hell!"

"I won't tell if you won't. Jealous?"

Yes. "No."

"Well, get after him. It's time to blow Fang Face away."

The engine roared as they raced up onto the highway. AV's bright red taillights weaved in and out of traffic about ten car lengths ahead.

"Looks like he knows we're coming." She changed lanes, pushing on the gas. "And don't you dare discharge your weapon. There are civilians everywhere."

Smoke rolled down the window. "Don't you have a siren or something?"

"No, Starsky, I don't."

A grin crept onto Smoke's busted lips. "Just pull alongside."

"What are you going to do?"

"Blow his doors off."

Barreling down the highway one lane over, Sidney caught up with AV.

"Perfect!" Smoke yelled.

AV slammed on his brakes.

The grenade blasted out of the barrel and tore out a section of the guard rail.

"You missed?" Sidney said.

"It happens." Smoke started firing short bursts of bullets. *Takka takka... takka takka...*

AV turned the Escalade off at the next exit.

"Great, he figured that plan out," she said, cruising after the SUV. She was three car lengths from the bumper.

"Get closer," Smoke said, shooting out the back windows. "I need to get the wheels."

"No," she said, "he might slam on the brakes."

"You're joking."

"No, wouldn't you do th—"

The SUV's brake lights blared. The huge car started to screech.

Sidney hit the brakes and slung the wheel over to the right. She hit the berm and skidded by until they came to a stop.

"Perfect," Smoke said, crawling out the window. He fired the launcher over the hood.

Toomph!

Inside the cab of the Cadillac, AV's fierce yellow eyes shone like moons. The entire front end of the SUV exploded.

Ka-Boom!

The front of the car was engulfed in flames.

"That ought to do it." She got out of her car.

Smoke approached the burning car and unloaded a few more rounds into it.

Takka takka... takka takka....

There was nothing left but a ball of flame and black

smoke. Smoke circled with wary eyes, barrel lowered toward the flames. The driver's side door opened with an eerie groan and fell onto the pavement.

AV the werewolf stepped out. All of his fur was smoking.

Smoke let him have it.

Takka takka... takka takka...

AV barked a wolfish laugh. "Fools, you can't kill me!" The werewolf's eyes narrowed on Sidney.

She went for the pistol as the monster closed in. She brought the weapon up and fired a blast into the ground where AV once stood.

Hurtling through the air, he landed on top of her. The breath was knocked out of her, and the pistol clattered over the road. AV wrapped his claws around her neck and squeezed. "Goodbye, Pretty!"

Crack!

AV's wolfish head jerked forward.

Smoke locked his rifle under AV's neck and pulled back with both arms. AV released his grip on Sidney.

Gasping for breath, she crawled away.

"Get the gun!" Smoke yelled.

The werewolf bucked and slung like a bull.

Smoke held on to the rifle and rode the werewolf like a cowboy.

Sidney searched for the pistol. A glimmer of metal rested underneath her tire. Snatching it up, she rolled to a knee and took aim. AV now had Smoke in a headlock.

"One shove," AV said, concealed behind Smoke's body, "and I break him. Walk away, and I'll let him live. I'll let both of you live."

She didn't have a clear shot. Little more than half of his head was exposed.

"Take the shot," Smoke sputtered. "You've got to take the shot and forget about me."

"Touching," AV said, applying more pressure to Smoke's head.

The large man's face turned purple. She heard bones popping and cracking.

Her eyes found Smoke's.

His lips spit out two words. "Center mass."

"Time's up, Pretty," AV said. He howled at the moon. "And I don't think you can hit me anyway."

In a burst of motion, Smoke shifted his leg behind the werewolf and flipped him over.

Sidney fired.

Blam!

Both men lay on the road, and only one of them started moving.

Smoke peeled the werewolf's arms off him. Hair, claws, and wolf face retracted. In seconds, Adam Vaughn was back, wearing only shorts made from spandex. He had a bullet hole in his heart. While examining the body, Sidney noted a strange brand on his back shoulder: a rising black sun that seemed to be bleeding.

"Good shot," Smoke said, groaning. "Can I have my gun back now?"

She started to hand it to him and stopped. "I have a question first."

"All right."

"How did you get your hands free, inside AV's office?"

"Diamond dust on my fingernails." He flashed his hands. Where there wasn't blood, they twinkled a little.

"Did you learn that in the SEALs?"

"No, it's from a Punisher comic book."

"Is that from the prison archives, Smoke?"

He smiled. "Finally."

EPILOGUE

THE NIGHT BECAME EVEN LONGER. Fire trucks arrived. Local law enforcement and the FBI followed. No one listened, and Smoke was back in handcuffs. Sidney spent an hour arguing her case, only to have Ted arrive in his brown trench coat and clear things up in five minutes.

"A werewolf?"

"Don't judge me, Ted." She yawned. She didn't really care if he believed it or not. At the moment she was happy to be alive.

"I know, but that corpse looks like a man." He watched the emergency crew bag AV up. "Next time take a picture. Maybe a video. And we wanted him alive."

"I tried. We both tried, sort of." She touched her lip and winced. "At least I don't have prom tomorrow."

"What?" Ted shook his head.

"Nothing. So what happens to him?" she said, looking at Smoke. He was sitting in the back of a police cruiser, all stitched up.

"Back to prison, I guess." Ted patted the hood of her

car. "Man, I can't believe you outbid me by a dollar. A dollar! The Hellcat sure is pretty."

Sidney wasn't paying much attention. Her thoughts were on Smoke, AV, deaders, the Black Slate... Many things. But mostly Smoke.

"Go home," Ted said, rubbing her shoulder. "Come in when you feel like it tomorrow."

A wrecker hauled the SUV off and the ambulance pulled out with AV's body.

"I'd rather head back to that hospital."

"Sid, there's a dozen agents over there already. Damned if we didn't find more missing children." He scratched his head. "What you did was a good thing. Another good thing. Take comfort in that. As for your friend, I'll do what I can."

An FBI agent shut the cruiser door on Smoke, got inside the car, and sped away. Her friend had vanished. Her chin dipped and she sighed. Then the rain came down.

The next day, stiff as a board, Sidney headed into the office. Five hours later, she turned in her statement of events to Ted. It was fifteen pages long.

"Geez, Sid." He put on his glasses. "It's just a report, not a bestseller."

She scanned the trophies, pictures, and colorful memorabilia on his wall. "What's the matter? Are you worried it might cut into football?"

"No. Well, yes." He huffed a breath and looked up

at her. "Sid, I'm sorry, and I want you to know that I'm glad you're all right. But deaders? What is a deader?" His desk phone rang. He picked it up. "Ted." His face darkened and he hung up. "Dammit." He picked up her report and grabbed his dress coat. "Got to go."

He was gone, leaving her all alone. She slipped out of his office, grabbed her bag, took the elevator, and went to her car. The old Interceptor. *At least it's not raining.* The rattle in the dash was even worse than before. She turned up the radio and headed for Mildred Bates hospital. Driving up the entrance, the first thing she saw was a great yellow crane with a wrecking ball. She pulled into the parking lot, parked, and got out, gaping.

The entire hospital was rubble. A dump truck loaded with debris rode by. The company name and logo, she instantly recognized.

Drake.

Her phone buzzed. A picture of her sister, Allison, and niece, Megan, popped up. The text below it read: Watch your step.

The Supernatural Bounty Hunter Files continue in March 2015 with *I Smell Smoke…*

ABOUT THE AUTHOR

Craig Halloran resides with his family outside his hometown of Charleston, West Virginia. When he isn't entertaining mankind, he is seeking adventure, working out, or watching sports. To learn more about him, go to: www.thedarkslayer.com

WORKS BY THE AUTHOR

THE SUPERNATURAL BOUNTY

HUNTER FILES
Smoke Rising
I Smell Smoke
Where There's Smoke
Smoke on the Water
Smoke and Mirrors
Up in Smoke
Smoke Signals
Holy Smoke
Smoke Out
Smoke 'Em

ZOMBIE IMPACT SERIES
Zombie Day Care
Zombie Rehab
Zombie Warfare

THE DARKSLAYER SERIES 1
Wrath of the Royals
Blades in the Night
Underling Revenge

Danger and the Druid
Outrage in the Outlands
Chaos at the Castle

THE DARKSLAYER SERIES 2
Bish and Bone
Black Blood
Red Death

THE CHRONICLES OF DRAGON SERIES
The Hero, The Sword and The Dragons
Dragon Bones and Tombstones
Terror at the Temple
Clutch of the Cleric
Hunt for the Hero
Siege at the Settlements
Strife in the Sky
Fight and the Fury
War in the Winds
Finale

You can learn more about The Darkslayer
and my other books at:
Facebook – The Darkslayer Report by Craig
Twitter – Craig Halloran

61303309R00119

Made in the USA
Middletown, DE
18 August 2019